A Clockwork Apple

A Clockwork Apple

Belinda Webb

burninghouse

First published 2008.

A Burning House book.

www.burninghousebooks.com

Burning House is an imprint of

Beautiful Books Limited
36-38 Glasshouse Street
London W1B 5DL

ISBN 9781905636174

9 8 7 6 5 4 3 2 1

Jacket design by Head Design.
Typesetting by Ellipsis Books Limited, Glasgow.
Printed in Great Britain by Mackays of Chatham.

WITHDRAWN

Dedicated to my Da
Thomas Valentine Webb
1948-2007

Much Loved
Much Missed

Athair, gra go deo

PART ONE

1

There is me, [Alex], and my three Grrrlz, Petra, Georgia, and Mid, Mid being really mid, which sometimes makes me mad, though I know tisn't really her fault, [Poor Cow!]

The four of us Grrrlz are dressed in the height of non-fashion. That is, over our *La Perla* (me midnight blue, Petra peach, Mid white and Georgia red) hand embroidered lingerie [a cut above *Provacateur*], we have identical overalls – like those once worn by mechanics – only we don't ornate our overalls with fake oil marks – like some of those saddo middling gringos.

Now, let me get this clear, once and for all, these are not jumpsuits, or catsuits, or anything of the sort – these are A1 grade authorentik mechanics' or engineers' overalls which, unlike those of a grease monkey man, we keep in impeccable nick.

3

And ours are khaki green.

The colour of the state sponsored fighter.

But we aren't sponsored by the state to fight, only by our own H.P.'s - to fight to honour our Phrontisteries. Or, at the very least, to avenge the dismissal and frustration of said Phrontisteries.

They are straight-legged – not boot cut, nor skinny like skinny snorting piggy wiggie old Moss now on the Side, nor flared like what is Madchester old skool 'student takeover pretending to be street' Hacienda days neither, nothing like that – just straight-legged; sitting comfortably over our racing-green ballet pumps which are great for peggin' down the streets in. Especially a long stretch of road like Oxford, peggin' our way down past the old picture house, past:

The Phoenix

Madchester Museum

City University No. 3 – Amis Campus

City University No. 4 – Eagleton Campus

Holy Name R.C. church (Theirmen, not ours)

sorry excuse of an art gallery which is The Whitworth and then

the body repair shop what is commonly known as the Madchester Royal Infirmary.

4

We never peg it farther than Wilmslow Road though, which is also known as the **Curry Mile** or what was once labelled The Muslim Ghetto.

We have a pocket over the left breasts of our mechanics, stitched round with a darker green – impeccable needlework it is. A little old man it waz who did it for us.

Us, needles?

Forgeddaboudit.

Those dayz is long gone, yeah.

The buttons that lead from the neck to the navel are hidden with an unmarked seam.

Great little workman. Collars are equally unadorned.

And our hair? *You have to ask.* We all wear our locks scraped back off of our faces with a dragon clip which also doubles as a slinky, shiny, sharp, silver blade – not cos it is fashion or anything like that, but because, like the ballet pumps and overalls, is more practical.

Besides, have you tried running with hair flapping on and off of your face? And those girls that saunter down a windy street, and their long flowing superstraight, or fashionably kinky hair that blows in their face – not just blowing, mind, but slaps them across it – **slap, slap, slap**, and she keeps on moving it out of the way so she doesn't walk into a lamp-post, but she doesn't fucking use her Phrontistery and tie it back – *they,* yeah, get on our wicks like nothin' else and so deserve the vilipend treatment. Letting their own hair whip their freshly trowelled faces, and who also, [like one of those annoying little yapping bag dogs *tsk tsk*], let their heels be bitten by shoes that go by the name of Fuck Me, or Fuck that! Or what the fuck ever.

We say, you wear Fuck Me, we say Fuck You.

Nuff said.

Mary Janes though, they, yeah, are worse.

No more shoe talk now though. *Only ballet pumps.* Without the fucking pirouette bollox, mind. *D'ya get me, lah?*

Get this!

Mid wants a zip on her mechanics, so she can, well, zip it down halfway or something, but Mid never has much of an idea of anysphinx, what wiv her being dead Mid and all that. But no, what we said is BUTTON IT RIGHT! Otherwize you can just forget it all, and that.

We sit in the Gutshot Rebos bar, wondering where to begin, like, on our dreams an' ambitions and all that - *d'ya get me?*

But!

It being Madchester and all, it is raining. And we aren't so girly that we carry cutie ickle brollie wollies around with us. *That.*

Right.

Just would not happen.

Ever.

Anyway . . .

I digress. The Gutshot Rebos bar specializes in the provision of health affirmative shots; for us that meanz wheatgrass, and a little spoon of an invigorating tonic, which kind of speedz up me and my sistaz' glorious Phrontisteries, that is, our **minds**.

Most of our fellow Gutshot Rebos patrons, girlies and boys alike, are loafing around reading, not **proper** stuff, but looking at pictures, tabloid barathrums that they are, like theyz still in the ickle wickle nursery school. Theyz hypnotised by pictures of girls and boys who have **made it** and who are saying with their new capped smiles, '*Look at me, aren't I clever, don't you want what I've got?*'

Me and my girlies, we sneer, yes, *sneer*, at these

picture gazers – hypnotised as they are by pix of people whose Phrontisteries are based on *nothing*, nish, zilch, *d'ya get me?* And then they look at the occasional headline **'Tallulah gets her new plastic tits out for the lads – again – page three'** [*hee hee haw haw*]. It is saying nothing more than, (in a big Essex accent) *aah, little Heidi's gone and done it again, what's she like, eh, eh!?*

Resounding *ha ha he he's* or *he he ha ha's*.

It is all widdershins, my dear sistaz, all widdershins.

We get another wheatgrass and dream tonic and allow ourselves to become our own little H.P., that is, not the sauce, but *the* source; the Power that is Higher, yeah, within ourselves.

We sit here, the four of us, in our regular little brown leatherette booth, connect with our own H.P. source and vilipend. We have little pennies or pounds on us. But, as they say, money isn't everything, a saying we choose to adopt simply because Jordon, skinny 'posh' Vikki *et al* are saying that it's everything. And they, yeah, are Detritus – with a capital **D**.

D'ya get me?

To us they are totally *De Trop*.

De TRIPE!

Anyway, there are three geezers sitting at the counter all together, as they do. But there is four of us Grrrlz and it is usually like **one for all** and **all four one**.

These big ed meatheads though, theyz dressed in the height of *their* fashion, which is most absolutely certainly no-way not ours. They have multi-coloured wiggies on their biggies – **see**, they sphinx they can have any bastard fing, but yet they cannot escape the old wiggie for their thinning biggies, pathetic pilgarlicks that they are.

Hee hee haw haw.

They also have the old eye-liner performing sideways brackets round their eyes. They wear these Turkish style black flarey shorts, proper divvie and all that, and they have these little gold episemons all over their star-trek wide shouldered jacket thingies. And wear big square 'orrible versions of what used to be known as Teddy shoes. Or somesphinx.

What is on these little gold episemons?

It is, dear Grrrlz, (hee hee) the miniature bedpost notches – each badge having like, the name of each, well, isn't no Grrrl that is for *sure*, more like . . . Fill in the blank yerself.

Anywayz, we is up for a bit and all that. Well, therez long term material, and therez short term material, and then therez 'don't even need to know their stinking names' material.

(Well, I'm not even sure they can be promoted to this latter level). But, they keep looking our way and a few of the Grrrlz look to me, yeah, as their high Leaderette, and then I nods, and they half-smiles, with a sneer on the side. *Lah.*

Proper snide.

And, being what they are, theyz go for the smile and ignore the sneer, meatheads that they are.

Predictable.

Anyway, like I sayz, we could do with a bit.

But the question is, my dear sistaz, am I yet **desperate** enough?

One of them deems us worthy enough to come over and leans his arm against the wall beside our booth. I nudge Petra.

'Power popper pricker,' she sayz.

We all do our meathead giggle wiggle. He looks at us all with suspicion glaring out of his brackets.

'Three of us, three of you, what say you little missies,' sayz he.

We sayz: 'hee hee haw haw'.

Mid looks at me.

I looks at her.

No need to say it. Punching way above his weight.

Petra looks at Mid.

Then Georgia.

We know who will be the contender for loser-outer.

Poor Mid.

Too mid for words.

But this guy, well he is just too dim for words, and dim, whilst being worse than dumb, is way much worse than mid.

'Anyway, bring 'em over, line 'em up then,' I sayz, petit tregateur that I am.

'Alright then doll,' he replies and rubs his hands together like a well-stocked shebeen owner in Prohibition. Well, I don't want to stray too far from the truth now, do I? Besides, this . . . meathead thinks he is some sort of Cock-a-knee bruiser with his 'alright then doll' crapola. So he dashes back to the counter and calls over his two mates who looks like theyz just been told it's Christmas, already anticipating the gleaming of new goldie looking episemons!

Anywayz, by the time theyz strollz, strutz,

saunters, whatever it is, over to our table, we have already got up and, noses high in the air we prance, yes *prance*, right out the door with a hey nonino and all that palaver. And no, no Grrrlz giggle. We don't need to.

'Here, love, here, come back, where ya goin'?' he calls, his poor meathead brain still locked onto what he deems to be a promise.

Hee hee haw haw. No badges for us. No Mid, no Alex, Petra or Georgia for display on their episemons! Foolz.

Nothin' less.

We are now speeded up proper stylee and our feet hardly touch the pissing wet grey manky Mancunian concrete, laid by too many poor Irishmen long before who knew nought of Conradh na Gaeilge. So, in

single
file
we
are
synched
in ballet pump
footsteps,
we glide,

glade,

gleed,

very glad

through Piccashitty gardens where theyz speak nuffink but Piccashitty Palare.

My arse!

Or rather, their arse!

Plural, not singular.

Too damn plural for us Grrrlz. Let em stick it up theirz.

Anywayz, seems like we aren't graceful or yare enough on our dolphin head like ballet pumps. For, there, behind us, are the three meatheads, CLOMPING, STOMPING, like little baby-men, but not through Piccashitty Gardens, for theyz can't bear it – too much of a strong reaction if you ask me, and people do. Frequently.

Anyhoo . . . like old Frankenstein's monster with the big old metal square boots, these silly-arsed baby-men, who can't take the old brush off from Grrrlz, are banging their big old plates of meat round the Gardens.

Well, we stop right there for 'em. We are ready. *D'ya get me, lah?*

All the hyenas in the Piccashitty Gardens begin

screaming and laughing like, well, yeah whatever
and all that. Worse than ickle girlie Blytons spouting
amphigory. These big ed meatheads stand there.
The three of 'em.

The farva

the son

and the unholy spirit.

Hee hee haw haw.

And we do what is right.

Fight!

Theyz will soon cancrizan right outta here.

We purse our unvarnished lips and spin around
with a kung-fuer that even that Gallic (*hauteur*)
legend footballing hero Cantona would have been
proud of.

And remember! There iz three of 'em, four of us,
so Petra sits out this particular dance to sweep back a
few stray curls that have escaped onto her forehead.

The hyenas continue their screeching amphigory,
then shout Palare at us, like theyz want us to join
their ranks as fag hags.

'Fuck that,' we sayz. We only on our own
ranks.

'Youse can shut it too,' I shoutz over. And theyz
shut up sharpish. Right and all. This ain't no Will

and Grace bollox. This is LIFE.

REAL.

And it's a war zone between us,

and them

and them,

and them,

and us and them,

EVERYONE who isn't a Grrrl and isn't prepared
to stand up and fight

with graceful ballet moves and,

more importantly,

with

WORDS.

Boustrophedon. Yep, both ways.

To write is to fight.

D'ya get me?

You will. Maybe not today, maybe not tomorrow . . .

So we carries on now, little graceful leaps above
the piss-stained, ever-wet Manky paving slabs,
leaving the boo-hooing hee hees behind us.

'Where to now Alex?' Petra asks as we all continue
in a half-jog, half leap

synchronised single-file sweep
down Portland Street.

'Just onwards, onwards, onwards,' I sayz, sounding
more like an old steam chug chug.

'We shall see what turns up,' Mid sayz.

'No, turns, not up, by the time it has turned, it
is up, then we shall see it, and not before, we cannot
see it in gestation, d'ya get me?' I sayz, playing
pedantry with the sophy peasantry. Yes dear reader,
Mid, whilst being mid and more than a tad Blyton,
is also the new peasantry, much as I don't want
her to be, she just is. Poor Cow!

Anywayz . . .

I digress, yet again. We find ourselves now, ten
minutes or so later, down by the old state television
centre, aka Auntie, for why, I know not, my auntie,
she definitely not, for it is not a she but a he.

We cut through Mrs. Gaskell Avenue for a little
detour, then down behind the Phoenix, towards the
old university where all the kids from the Blyton
district are sent to be trained on how to boss us
around and all that.

We then find ourselves on Burns Street, named
after Saint Engel's old bit of fluff. But long term,
mind, although she got no credit for his ancient book

on the old poor peasantry of this still pissing grey city.

We don't mind him.

The General is what the old war men called him.

Anyhoo . . . we are too tempted by the large wrought iron railings of the Amis Campus and we do what we always end up doing. We all leap up at the bars, like the urban cheeky monkeys that we are. As always the screech screech screeching of the alarm tells all and sundry that the University is UNDER ATTACK. We allow ourselves a few more gymnastics and then jump up and off. The yellow light has begun to reign over us, follow us, until we run across the road, take shelter in some bushes and watch the little drama-rama unfold. Always the same. Two big meatheads in blue uniforms come stamping out, their stamping and jutting forward of their flashlights no different from the scared little boy's whistling in the dark to keep up his spirits. Theyz turn off the yellow beam and siren, yet continue to aim their own laser lights in all directions except the one we are in – hee hee haw haw. I had the highly unfortunate experience of being 'caught' by one of those laser lights once

– like a stun gun and MACE in one. Not that I've had either.

Yet.

But I imagine. Of course I do, if you know anything about me by now, it's that.

It should be.

And so do you.

And, my dear sistaz, if you don't, continue no more.

This is a journey. Much more than a trip.

Anyway, we continue to wait, hunched down in the bushes. Mid pulls off a few leaves and fondles them between her fingers, remembering. We don't got much greenery in Moss-Side, see. Georgia pulls out a thin lock of her hair and twiddles it around her finger, pulling it, curling it, letting it go, pulling it, curling it, letting it go – just like I sometimes like to do when I'm reading. My mumsy wumsie, more on her later, believe me, if you knew her now, as I do, there'd be no rush, she went through a phase, if that's what you can call four and a half years, when she would do nought but pull her hair, curl it, let it go, then grab it, tease it, then PULL IT OUT! And I would sit in the kitchen and watch clumps of hair hit the ground. An extreme form of escapism from present reality, no? Or just the plain regular old brand of self-loathing? Enough! They have gone. Petra is picking at her nails, anxious, waiting, needing to expel the built-up energy, as built-up as our urban structures, and strictures. We are about to leave when I spy a figure emerging from one of the gothic side doors, from which I had always imagined the last person to leave would have been someone like Eagleton himself, carrying the manuscript of his own brand of Ideology. Trying to work it out. And failing. And flailing. They all do. Eventually, my dear sistaz, they all do. That is why authorenticity and expression is so important. This figure trundles a few yards down Oxford Road, yet, before Medical Research Building No.5, she turns left. Petra nudges me. I nudge Petra. D'ya get me? We slink out and about. Like slinky cats of the night.

Pad

        Leap

Then . . .

POUNCE!

Just as she is about to escape into her three-wheeler. It is a her. And she is old. Wearing half-moon glasses. I mean, who wears them any more? All those lasers are legion and having to hold up apparatus over the eyes by way of the nose! Like wearing the old La Perla *over* the overalls – what use? Now, I has to tell you, my dear sistaz, this is not a common sight. No, not at all, what wiv the ANGER and all that. And she has a box in her hand. Put a bow on it and it could be a gift! Well. It's mine. Gift or no.

'Oh! Give it back, come on, do give over, and give it back.' She pleads.

'Pardon ME, *sister*,' I sayz back, right in her wrinkled face. It reminds me of an overlooked garden whose petalled faced adornments had been taken over by nought but straggledy weeds.

'What is it? How can I help you?' she asks, in one of those loud middling, artificially glass cut voices that tries to convey itself as wooly minded liberal who really thinks it's boheme. But I detect a trace of Oz there, somewhere. 'Now listen, I understand . . .' she begins.

Yes, I think, yes, you THINK you do, you think you understand, pre-empting my little speech.

'Shut up, you've had the voice for long enough, LONG. ENOUGH,' I shoutz.

'Yes, well . . .' she sayz now in a wibbly wobbly voice, realizing what an imbroglio she is in.

Hee hee haw haw.

I open the box. I have to say, I like the sound of the lid inching its way off. I wack the lid over Mid's head. 'OW!' she sayz, rubbing her head. We all laugh. But then, there in the box, what is there, my dear sistaz? What's in the box? Well, it's a . . . a . . . shiny, gold notebook. A golden notebook.

'So, I see you have some book here then, strange sister,' Petra sayz.

'Shut it Petra,' sayz I, 'the words here are *mine*, and mine alone, d'ya get me?' I am beginning to feel twitchy.

'Aye,' she replies.

'Yes, a book, and gold too,' she sayz, and she attempts to grab it. I slap her hand away. I take the book out of the box. The box falls to the floor with a THUD. I hold the book up. The moon, half full, reflects itself in its surface. Mid, Petra, and Georgia are, for a second-o transfixed.

'Let me show you,' old Oz woman sayz.

'No! Let *me* show you!' sayz I.

I opens the book and am immediately taken by small, minute, ink-scripted handwriting. I look

21

closely in order to decipher the text.

'But no, there are some wonderful sketches in the back, here, let me show you,' Oz woman sayz, and her poor shaky hands inch towards the book. I get the book and immediately WHACK it against her smooth knuckles that look as though theyz never seen a bucket of hot water and detergent.

'OW!' She cries.

'Shut. Up.' Georgia demands, in that final tone of voice that she has. She doesn't say much, does our Georgia, but when she does, she does. D'ya get me?

'It is some sort of enchiridion, is it not?' I asks. This perplexes her far more than the WHACK against the knuckles. Theyz don't like it, see, don't like you flying out of the pigeon hole to which they have, automatically, stuffed you in.

'An en-en-enchiridion? Yes, yes, that's what it *was*, still is . . . I guess . . . but look, you see, I have much better books, books full of colour pictures and . . .'

'I see what you is doing, trying to get us into that hypnotic trance like the rest of the tabloid barathrums, well, we ain't interested in 'em. No. Words, that's us, you used to be into them yourself, didn't you, you little germ you,' I sayz.

She looks at me, frightened, like a poor wragged single mum whose little child is throwing a tantrum in the old hypermart, and who won't respond no more to the bribery of sugar sticks. She just screams the whole fucking place down. Well, she is our natural little sister, that screaming, demanding child throwing a tantrum in the hypermart, who refuses to be fobbed off anymore with sugar sticks and dollie wollies with yellow hair. We smash the sugar sticks to the floor. And the dollie wollies with the yellow hair? We cover their faces in ink, then pull the heads off their plastic bodies and slam them against the nearest wall, pretending it's everyone else.

'Well, I could read some of the other pages for you, yes, I could do that, would that help, mmmm? Wouldn't you like to know what the words are?' she now asks, desperately changing tack.

'No, you germ you, it will not, and furthermore, however, moreover, old missey, you're assuming one insultive, offensive thing here, in what you just said, you're assuming me and my Grrrlz here can't read.

Well, WE CAN!' You are not worthy even to be my famulus. Nor even my amanuensis.

Hee hee haw haw.

Her eyes become fixed on my face. The pigeon has flown out of its coop and is headed for a strange place, far far away. She nearly chokes on her own rapidly forming spittle of fear. That's when she realises; the penny drops that maybe, just maybe, we know.

'And, erm, have you, have you read . . .' she begins.

'Yes. We have, all that about eunuchs and Shakespeare's Wife and the second-best bed . . . no, now listen, what now? Where are we, my sistaz?' I turns and askz my Grrrlz.

They shrug their shoulders.

I turns back to oldey worldey woman and shrug my shoulders with all the emphasis of one who lives only for impression management and who knows nothing of the saying 'To thine ownself be true'.

'I know, I know, I'm sorry, not enough action, I know, too much wordey type things . . .' she begins, trying to get each word out as fast as she can.

'Yes, oldey worldey woman,' sayz I, action is

Queen, and you failed to worship the Queen, the High Priestess, and now look at us – we've only just escaped from the meatheads with their plates of meat who are more like Wells' warlocks.'

She nods her head quickly. I place the enchiridion inside my overalls. I massage my hands.

'Oh no. Well. D-d-d-don't hurt me too bad, I have problems with my joints now you see . . .' she sayz.

'Oh dear, listen you germ of a . . . man.' Everyone takes a sharp intake of breath.

'We ain't gonna do nish, action yes, but not this, d'ya get me?'

She nods again, but I know she doesn't – get me that is. Could she ever? Too Blyton femme by half.

We thinkz we should hold a bonfire with her tits holder upper, but it doesn't look like she had ever worn one. Tsk Tsk. We are on our way, my dear sistaz, on our way. We continue the journey, leaving the oldster far behind. Speeded up nicely. But not before I shoutz back over my shoulder:

'You didn't shout loud enough for long enough. Now we're angry, NOW WE'RE ANGRY NOW!
WE!

ARE!
ANGRY!'
And The Gutshot Rebos special has kicked in nicely. But the evening, my dear Sistaz, has only just begun.

We darts off down Oxford, down McColl, then down Thatcher street, where, there, in the heart of the Blyton students' utilities and provisions district, is our intended target.

A shoe shop going by the highly original name of HEEL! Like, yeah, we'd heel for it alright. We look at each other. Knowing. Glinting. Gleaming.

Georgia takes out a long, thin piece of wire. Mid smiles and then climbs onto Petra's waiting lowered palm. While she supports her, Mid does what she is good at – cutting the wires of alarms. That done, Georgia takes the wire and unlocks the door.

Hey Presto!

The shop has come to HEEL!

Ours.

We sneak in, take off our ballet pumps and line them up, as neat as a Japanese family of four, by the door. From the window display I take a pair of the best boots – complete with pointed and razor sharp FUCK ME heel.

'Fuck you!' Sayz I.

To who?

To 'them'.

Mid runs into the store room and fetches back three additional pairs of the same. I watch and wait with satisfaction as theyz each slip their balletic feet into the boots.

Bovver? No, my dear sistaz, not for us – only for the *other*.

Our ballet pumps we take and carry with us, one in each hand. We exit and stand in front of the large plate glass window which hardly any other has for the too obvious temptation theyz hold to smash to smithereens, so obvious they are of the ANGER, yet not wanting to CONFRONT it.

'READY?' I ask. They all nod, with arched eyebrows. I give the order:

'NOW!'

We each hold out our arms, like we wuz on the cross or somesphinx, which of course we are, if one thinks about it philosophically, which most no longer do.

Then! Sticking to our ritual, we each, in synch, lift our right legs halfway, pull back and crash the heel into the window.

My dear sistaz, what a lovely bullet-hole type wound it has made. We crunch our heel in and around, like a Japanese Samurai sword wanting to make sure all internal organs are spliced not once,

twice,

but thrice.

NICE! Satisfaction.

Then we pull out *THEIR* heel and OUR legs and place both our arms back by our sides, like gymnasts who have just completed a vault exercise and have already paraded their non-existent chests to the judges and audience.

We each examine our heel mark – for, my dear sistaz, it is just like the Star of the East, what wiv the not full shilling luney planet shining just in the right place. A 'sign', perhaps, some would say. No?

This is our star, our stars, and we follow the anger that leads us to create in this way.

Create? I hear you ask.

Yes, create.

Our lives are art. Or rather, we have learned to turn our anger, not on ourselves, but on IT.

The world.

And so we create.

For there is nothing else to do; nothing else to be done. This is our Expression – and it is *Queen*.

What, my dear sistaz, is life for, if it cannot allow expression? And not prescribed expression either. Prescribed expression? Like the great bearded one who has, even now, to remain unnameable for fear of didacticism, and false crudity charges, and yet whose words spoke to this city and its Chartists like no other, one time; we would turn crimson at the prospect of prescribed expression – prime example of oxymoronia.

We march,

two x two this time,

always two x two in the old FUCK MEs,

to

       the next one

          along.

It is not shoes this time, my dear sistaz, but nuclear gadgets, that, whilst be new, are nowhere near clear. Its own window display is of a cut out man from some distant age – yeah, like, this shop is trying to get in on the nostalgia route, some slicker in slacks and combed back hair, and in one hand he holds the latest bit of gadgetry that no one needs – at least, not until they are TOLD theyz need it and then shamed by their peers if they don't part with their money for it. Blasted ghastly sheep-like Blytons!

'Tosser,' sayz I.

Yes, dear sistaz, I know it is not a real OTHER, but it is an actor what did it - so to speak, someone who makes a very good living out of false impression management.

D'ya get me? Lah. Of course you do. You should. By now.

Anyways, we are about to go through the same ritual but with the opposite side.

The left side.

Arms out – we are ready to fly. Left leg raised off the ground and then up and IN, another set of four stars. We looks at each other and SCREAM.

Then we take the boots off, put our comfy pumps back on, return to HEEL! and line up our borrowed boots outside the door.

Having expressed ourselves artistically and communally we then skip, *yes skip, leap over bollards, climb up and over old derelict boxes which used to hold telephones and texting contraptions and demolish an advertising screen, FISTS this time, not FEET.*

A few leaps and jumps until it occurs to me that we had better drop in on our mumsy wumsies in the Old Duchess of New York on McColl Street. It is just by the side of the old bodyshop MRI. Nice and handy for the old mumsie wumsies, see, theyz frequently get careless what with the amount of poison they ingest – *Gutshot Rebos for them is like McDonald's for a veggie.*

And sure enough, there in the snug, sitz the four muvvaz.

Muvvaz my arse! Of the word's import theyz know nish.

Now, my dear sistaz, you must allow me the honour of introducing this kenspeckle of cackles:

There is Holly, who is Petra's old muvva, and she is indeed very spiky, but without the softening of red berries.

Then there is Kylie, who is Georgia's muvva, who is a bit of an old Irish traveller tinker type, with goldie looking earrings and all, that drags her drooping earlobes almost down to her equally drooping shoulders. I say Irish, but it is more of a hybrid of who-knows-what.

Then there is Gloria, that's Mid's old muvva, who is anything but glorious.

Then there is Sharon, that's me own muvva. Less said about that old lush the better.

But she nudges Kylie and pipes up into her well-worn Jeremiad:

'Ooh! Look what the wind's blown in, now piss off girls, don't be coming in here mithering us, we've 'ad it 'ard we 'ave.'

They all nod and in synch take a sip of their stoutish mixtures which theyz would take guttatim by and by, and make sure IT IS every guttatim, too.

'Aaah, mumsie wumsies 'av 'ad it 'ard, has theyz?' I whines, to giggles from the Grrrlz. 'Yeah, leave it out,' I sayz, in my best mock Essex accent. This we always do when we are extracting the waste liquid out of anyone.

'Oh do shut it mummykins,' Mid sayz, which really quite surprises me, but then, she is always trying to remove herself from the narrow middling gone wrong background. Georgia snaps her fingers at the poor spotty yoof student male behind the old wooden counter that, *surprise surprise*, sports more blade marks than the bodies of most Moss-Siders. He comes running over.

Running over he comes.

His hands theyz a-shaking. Not only is he from Blyton, (we have a radar bladar for that sort of thing you see), but he is the opposite of the old meatheads, so I s'pose theyz each cancel out the other.

If only.

'Gis four waters for your four favourite aquabibs,' sayz I.

'Oh, here we go, comin' in here with the old water nonsense, listen girls . . .'

'GRRRLZ,' shouts Petra.

'GIRRRRLLLLZZZZZZZZZTHEN!' roars Gloria. I swear her voice sounds like custard dragging itself over pebbles.

'Now now, calm down, calm down,' sayz Mid.

'*Well!* Comin' in 'ere talking to your muvvaz like that, don't you know we gave birth to you lot? Do you know what we went through . . . ripped apart and stitched back up I was . . .' my old muvva begins.

'Oh do shut it up muvva dearest, what you always fail to overlook, that is, totally look over and deny, is that you CHOSE it, so SHUT IT. Now listen, we didn't come here to trash or to be trashed . . . is that clear?'

'But what are you so ANGRY about, eh? WHAT?

WHAT ARE YOU SO ANGRY ABOUT?'
Gloria shouts, ANGRILY.

I sigh a deep sigh, run a finger across the smooth arch of my left eyebrow, roll my eyes up to the ceiling and back. If I have to tell them once I have to tell them a thousand times.

'Asking what it is that we are angry ABOUT is to miss the point entirely,' said I. 'Anger is not *about* . . . It is MOURNING, the unknown, the loss of what went before without you, etcetera, etcetera, it's grieving is what it is, it's pining mumsy dearest, pining, only you and other Miss Understood's call it whining, and until Morning Has Broken, it shall continue ad infintium until ad nauseum.

D'ya get me, lah?'

'Do I get YA?! Do WE get ya? No! We only gave you to the world, and you've done nothing but throw a toddler's temper-tantrum ever since,' my old muvva sayz, before letting her slightly hairy top lip seek solace in the drink that is as stout as her always sitting arse.

'Cheeky kidz, cheeky, too much back chat by half,' Gloria sayz.

'Too right. By half. They are that,' me old muvva sayz.

Anyway. We turns to the bar. I sip a few sips of my aqua. I see Mid. She nudges Petra. I pretend not to notice. What she is up to, I do not know. But I will. As always. I will. She does seem to be taking her peep-holes for too long a tour over the stained glass type bottles exposing themselves on the shelves behind the bar. Now that, to take a sip further in that direction, my dear sistaz, would be a step too far! And Mid, Petra and Georgia know that. Or rather, they should. By now. If they should know one thing by now, it's that. And if they do not, then theyz're not right in the hat. But temptation no more.

'Come, my Grrrlz, it's time to pound pavements once more . . .' But before I go I jump up on a chair, take a bow, and leap across tables, before leaving the old miasma of muvvaz to it. Georgia follows me out.

'Where are them two?'

'Mid's just popped in for a tinkle,' she sayz, but not meaning tintinnabulation. But, my dear sistaz, it is too late, I am suspicious. But I leave it. An old bus stop beckons and, whilst we wait, like dum dums, for Mid and Petra to appear, me and Georgia jump up on facing bars of the old shelter's metal frame and allow our bodies to stretch. I feel my shoulders release almost from their sockets, then find their homes again. I swing in. And out. And in. And out. Waiting. Angria and angria. They appear. Mid has a flush to her face. Petra looks slightly petulant, yet sheepish at the same time. No matters. Time will tell, for Mid lies unwell.

Blyton is the land of childish endeavours at childish times, somesphinx we are totally unfam with, might as well be a district of Eskimos. These kiddos are brought up with an awareness of Freud – familial conditioning and all that. What we need, where we come from, is more Erich Fromm, perhaps. Freud would be razored to death for his shameful ignorance of societal structures.

Do you know, when I read of Bronte's Angria adventures I immediately understood.

Stood under.

THUNDER!

The anger of their father's welly burning incidents.

Their own.

We knew. We know.

We saw. We see. Despite the time gap.

Angria was – is timeless. It always will be. The angria destroyed Branwell the boy. But only made Charlotte, Emily and Anne stronger, before extinguishing them all together. They ran rings of rage around Austen. For sure. For Austen was a Blyton Bore!

The land of angria took our own men.

Either turned them into useless meatheads or slivers of who they should have been.

They let go, ergo, they had to be let go of.

We wuz on our own.

Just as our muvvaz had been.

But we aren't going to be like them either.

EVER!

The thought is enough to give one nightmares.

And we aren't going to fall into the trap of justifying personal horrendousness with theory either, like De Beauvoir.

Fuck that!

Fuck them!

Fuck them all!
But keep self to self. Keep the anger pure and push it out against them – *they* created it – they can damn well take it.

Our muvvaz had taken it against themselves.

We're not gonna.

We are sacred.

And we will not be told otherwise.

NO FUCKING WAY.

We are about to move ahead as a quartet when a tranche of truncheon bearing women pull up to the kerb.

'What is this going on here then?' one of them, looking more like the Ironified Iron Lady of Mumpsimus herself, asks.

'What does it look like?' sayz I, waving my arm around like the Empress herself.

'Yeah, what does it bloody look like, eh?' sayz Georgia whose eyes dagger through the inquisitorial eyes of the authority figure. Nihilists all of us, for we know their own specialization is that of ultracrepidation.

Thank the stars for that, eh?

'Where've you girlies been this evening then?' she demands, lips pursed to show the lines of a hard smoking habit.

'Been? Why, here, only here, what do you mean been?' I asks.

Mid gigglez, as she is wont to do when nervous; sometimes she really tests the limits of what it is to be a Grrrl! I throw her a look, which she catches sharpish.

'Have you?' the state authority woman asks.

'Well, who are you asking?' I asks her, trying to catch her snide peep-holes on something or someone in particular, seeing that she's trying to convey some secret code to Mid.

'You, you used to be a Blyton,' she sayz, shouting to the barman, whose hands are now well and truly in a tizz.

'And?' she repliez.

'Have you done anything this evening that you should come clean about right this minute, for we'll find out, oh yes, we will, we do, we always do.'

Well, my dear sistaz, she's asked twice; because of that perhaps we should come clean and admit to our authorenticity of action. They really are from some other planet.

'Done? Nothing done,' Mid repliez.

She stares at her, trying to determine whether

this ex-Blyton is capable of being a tregateur. Theyz don't want to believe it, you see, not of Mid! And yet, they don't realise that, whilst Mid keeps a secret part of herself forever Mid, that we do know, they also don't see that there is another part of her that will never forgive her own for the dissing of illusionment upon which she had been brought up before Moss-Side.

'Right then, well, make sure you stay out of trouble,' she warns, then, giving one last hard steely stare into each of our faces, more particularly into my own, (if truth be known I think she's a dyke who only has infatuations with either undecided or straight, shame none of us Grrrlz fit into either of those categories, for we are non-participants if truth be known, aka asexual and before you start thinking repression and Freud think again) and I smilez back at her.

She half smilez those pursed lips and marches away, followed by her famulus wannabes, who each, in turn, attempt the same growling look, not realizing it could never work to any effect, even in a Moss-Side growlery, for theyz only achieve a kind of spastic like lack of control of facial features.

It is, my sistaz, an attempt at impressions management gone mad.

Hee hee haw haw.

But, despite having spent some of our Grrrl power from the land of Angria, there is still plenty in the bank, so to speak – everything to fight against.

Really.

And the night is still very young.

2

We contine apace down the not so bracing polluted air of McColl Avenue.

'Come on then Grrrlz, let's walk, and talk, and keep our little beady ones wide open,' sayz I. And so we pace ourselves after our little hour or so of excitement. We find ourselves back on Oxford Road, which is not the road to Oxford, or, for us, not even Cambridge, or Madchester itself – ha ha ha, funny innit! Like I sayz, that is still, in this day and age, for the Blyton lot. We, you see, are from the opposite of the side of moss, that is, Moss-Side, where one time a fantasist of an author grew up.

Anyway sistaz, our eyes all zone in on a huddle of . . . holding onto each other as they pass the old big Dickensian body shop, that is, the MRI. This group, sensing us (you see, the streets are mainly empty most of the times), turnz.

'STOP!' I shoutz.

The figures freeze and emit a woeful whimper.

'Where are you going?' asks I, like I am the boss of the world, which even I know I could only ever dream of being. Anywayz, we take a few paces forward and find ourselves in front of this group of women, which is what they would be optimistically categorized as in the old bodyshop behind us.

Another group of drunkies. Someone's mumsie wumsies no doubt. 'Alright darlin'?' one of them asks. Another one, her arms linked on either side, is so far gone that, if she was let go by the other two, would simply fall to the floor and there stay. Her eyes roll around her head. Streams of sick have run dry all the way down her chin and down her neck to where, god knows.

'I aint your fakkin' darlin,' sayz I in me best Essex. The three Grrrlz begin to laugh. No, actualie, theyz didn't begin to laugh, theyz *do* laugh, see, you either laugh or you don't, even when it's a creeping gesture, inching its way, creeping across your face, like a sly slugaroo.

Mid lunges forward and gives her a kick in the old shins. She, that is the old drunkie, screams in a way that only an old woman can.

Half cackle. Hackle?

She launches back into the galimatias of filthy old songs of her muvvaz that we have so rudely interrupted.

'Muvvaz, my arse!' shouts I. She stops, and so too, through no choice, all the others.

'You've got a mother too,' she announces, as though it is a NEWSFLASH! 'You have, we all have, howd'ya think we gots 'ere, eh?' she asks. And, I swear to you, my dear sistaz, she has tears in her eyes now, despite her earlier songs of drunken bravadaccio. But I am relentless. I cannot be otherwise. Yet.

'Anyone can plop one out,' sayz I, 'it's not as if they have a choice, once it's bin there a certain length of time, well, they have no choice, do they? What's so fucking virtuous and noble about it, eh, old bitch? Tell me?'

'TELL ME!' I screamz.

Not like me to lose control like this – screaming I mean, I'M USUALLY Queen of haecceity, upon which the realization of my individual existence

depends. But I now feel like a deranged opera singer
– Callas/Callous.

'You'll be muvvas youselves one day, then you'll
see how bleedin' 'ard it is, yes, you will! Now if
you're gonna hurt me, *us,* then do it. Go on! We'll
only end up in there anyway,' she sayz, pointing to
the old body shop behind her, 'you can't hurt us
more than we've already been hurt.'

She then weeps, whines and whinges.

Eeek! Another jolly Jeremiad – oh, my dear sistaz,
if this is all I thought we had to look forward to I
would end it all NOW.

'Oh do shut up oldie,' sayz I. 'Too many bitches
bitchin,' I sayz.

'WHY SHOULD WE?' she screams back at me.

'Becoz it's pathetic.

HELP! PLEASE HELP! HELP ME! IT'S A
CRY FOR HELP, PLEASE!'

The Grrrlz now laugh even harder.

I take a few steps forward, and so end up right in
front of this woman's face. The old bitch flinches.

'Do you know *why* you're stuck in your Jeremiad?
Because you
      were failed
      by

YOUR

MUVVA!

You and yours are stupid bitches – still crying for the moon, *see*? But now you is destined to cry for the moon. Stuck. If your cries for help had been seen to, well, you'd be alright, see?'

I don't know, my dear sistaz, it's as if my heart is trying to . . . fuck off, I don't know do I?

Don't know everything.

Not yet anyhow.

'GET YOURSELVES AWAY AND OUT OF THIS MESS YOU STUPID OLD . . .!' I shoutz.

The Grrrlz all jump back. Must have been louder than usual.

The group move forward, inching their way, staggering a little less, pulling harder on the arms of the sick stained eyeball roller.

'Yes, yes, we're going, we're going now,' she sayz, her voice strained but now sounding more sober than even a judge – which, like, isn't that fucking hard, is it? And off they scurry, down the road. We watch on, as the main one struggles to unlock her arm from the others, and wipes her old face hose on her holey sleeve.

We cross the deserted road and pass the old Whitworth sorry excuse of an art gallery that had only been built for the benefit of the Blytons.

We enter the darkened Whitworth Park, once the old raping ground of the red light walkers. I smile to myself, a smile of triumph, of daring, let one of the fuckers leap out the trees at ME! At US! They'd get the shock of their lives – they wouldn't even live long enough to feel the shock. I dare them, will them, silently. But, once you walk with daring, with fight, with *fire* in your belly, the fuckers don't wanna know. Cowards, all.

'Wouldn't it be good if someone jumped out at us now, eh?' I sayz. We all have a good belly laugh. Except Mid.

She is the only one who isn't laughing.

'Hey Middling Middie, have you allowed your noggin to become infected by the nation?'

Petra and Georgia look aghast, yes, *aghast* (Blyton word) at their fellow Grrrl.

She shakes herself out of it.

'Eh? No, course not.'

'No room on this path for those who belong in the herd, Mid,' I warn.

We continue our evening stroll until we come
out at Denmark Road and cross to the back of
what was once known as the Robin Hood, an old
type pub place, most of which are now heavily
guarded and regulated.

'The greatest good for the greatest number . . .'
Mid sayz, apropos of nothing, her eyes become
glazed again.

'What?' I asks.

Georgia punches her in the arm.

'OW!' she shoutz.

'WAKE THE FUCK UP!' I shoutz. She has fallen
into the land of the herd again and raises her face
up to the sky. We three look up to the sky and are
greeted by the half moon.

'She's halfway to looney tunes, that's all folks!'
sayz I. 'MID!' I bellows into her ear, the right one,
and punch her forearm.

'WHAT?' she asks, as if just woken up from a
beautiful slumber wumber.

'You're turning into one of the herd, is that what
you want?' She looks aghast. (That word again).

'NO! OH NO! OH MY GOD . . . WHAT IS
HAPPENING TO ME?' she screams, both hands
on her face like *The Scream*. A picture that is,

like, O.K. as it sayz more about the true state of affairs than Jordon and her army of plastic-tit wonders.

'YOUR GOD!' Petra shouts.

'No, no, not my god, like, oh, my god, as in, oh shite alight,' she screams, her voice all wibbly wobbly woo woo. She panics.

'Keep the fire in yer belly Mid, keep the fire, have you got it?' I ask, but knowing that what she wants is something a bit stronger than a shout in the ear. She looks to the old tarmac covered cobblestones, as if that is where her belly is kept, on the floor, and a light comes on in her eyes. She looks up at each of us in turn, like one of those saddos who's just been converted to born again Christianity. I take a step back. I isn't sure which world she is in now. What is her ontological landscape?

'The Fire, Grrrlz, is back in me belly, well and truly flaming, like the old Etna, like the first night of Guy Fawkes.'

We all smile.

'Don't lose it again you stupid mare,' sayz I. I am, I admit, an ickle bit worried. O.K. I thinks, perhaps Mid doesn't have as big a reservoir of fire in her belly than us.

No, I am not fucking saying that we has got bigger bellies like, but that it is an issue of the old social conditioning.

As without so within.

Well, for the first half of her life old Mid had been brought up in the safety of Blyton and then had to move to Moss-Side. ***Then*** she developed the fire. But we've had the fire raging since the day we were conceived in our test tubes.

'Nuff now, let's go!' I shouts. We have only just stepped onto Great Western Street when a cop car creeps up on us from nowhere.

Like, NOWHERE! Seriously, yeah. After us again. Never leave us be.

There is no way we are going to stand there and answer their baloney old questions of humiliation that have zilch to do with zeteticism. They'll only find something to take us in over, like how we couldn't possibly have been indoors watching Recovery Hour at the compulsory hour, and thus breaking the rule of state unity.

We pegz it across the road. The cop car has an orgasm for itself, delighting in what is going to be a chase. We are there – *yare,* and sprintz down Upper Lloyd Street.

But how to outrun a car? It comes level with us.

One of the policewomen orders her window down and shoutz:

'SLAGS! STOP NOW!'

Now, there's one thing I've always believed. You have to TRY and get people to treat you the way you think you deserve to be treated. Well, what message would I be sending to my poor old esteem should I respond to that call? It would be like me actually half believing that I is, or indeed could be, a slag. So we continue to leap through the sky, well, near enough.

Mid starts laughing. Nerves. Again.

I'm wondering if it was ever a good idea poaching her from Milly Molly Bandy's Girlies.

Petra and Georgia are never any problem. There has, so far, never been any question that we are of the same ilk.

There had never been any question.

They have the same fire in their belly. The fire to be oneself, regardless.

We jump over walls, fences and bollards and eventually outwit the old dum dums. I knew I should have been a gymnast. Anyway, we are somewhat out of breath, and yet we are in Blyton. Mid's old stomping ground. She is no longer too teary eyed about it. No missee. She looks around with disdain, disgust, diss . . . whatever, yeah. She hates them now just as much as we do. We hope.

We find an old car.

Well, we lie, we lie. 'Tis a new car. Rather yare too, just like us. Well, my dear sistaz, as you know, we have been exerting our limbs quite a lot this evening, time for a little comfort – a little of the old speed – not that we haven't had enough already.

Hee hee haw haw.

Petra does her long wire trick. Alarms have nowt on us. *D'ya get me?* I gets into the driving seat and does him up nicely and he purrs like a dream. A racy black number. Mid sits in the back with Georgia. Petra sits in the front with me.

Petra shouts, 'Bittersweet Symphony,' a piece of the old classical. And on it comes. And we sing along:

'Trying to make ends meet, you're a slave to the money – then you die.'

And we find other glorious old tunes. And have ourselves a great little sing-a-long. And the fire in our bellies gets hotter and hotter. But, not knowing too much about the old speed monsters the car goes on strike in the middle of nowhere, or so it seems – though we are probably no farther than Cheshire.

Ugh! *Cheshire.* Even the name sends shivers of disgust down my spine.

Cheesy.

Churches.

Cheerful chats.

Cheshire cats.

It is CHIT!

And now this car is BANG! BANG! We get out and I kicks the car door, hurts my foot and shouts, 'bastard car.' The Grrrlz giggle.

We walk down a now very dark countrified lane. We reach a house. Small regular cubes of light shine out. In the front garden there is a big fat sign, as proud as an obese Stetson-wearing Texan Christian evangelist.

It sayz:

'SERENITY'.

Hee hee haw haw, I sphinx. But there is a jingle of Cheshire chit-chats emanating from the back. So round the back we toddles.

In this, like, oasis of a garden there is indeed a group of Blytons. All stood around, glasses in hand, WINE BOTTLES abound. Chin-Chin, one of them calls. Oh, ha de ha ha ha, I thinks. Alright for them. They can, they think, control their consumption. It's just everyone else that can't, and thus they take their snippety sips and contribute to the order everyone else has to live under. They. Make. Me. SICK.

'Yes?' a man's voice calls over, his mouth is drop-of-wine-smiley, whilst his eyes are 'what the fuck are you doing HERE'.

'Please sir,' sayz I in my bestest babyish Blyton-esque voice, 'we've become a tad lost, wondering if you could help us.'

The Grrrlz giggle.

Lowly.

'Oh! I see. Well,' he sayz. This cheerful cheesy chit-chat group has quietened down and now observes this scene before them. A group of Grrrlz at the bottom of their idyll, at this time of the evening.

Then we hears this billy goat gravel-gruff voice from the group. 'What on earth, Derek, why don't you just tell them to shuffle off,' sayz he.

Oh fuck off, you plonker, I sphinx, but don't say. Yet. Derek, for that is his name, comes closer to us.

'From where?' he asks.

'From where what?' Georgia asks.

'From where have you become lost?' he asks.

'Do you really want me to answer that?' I replyz. A slight giggle from us Grrrlz. His slight smile drops. He wants to know what our private joke is.

A chiffon of lavender from an orderly row of the biggest candles I have ever seen trails towards us. But we don't mess around. No, not us.

We pushes him backwards and run rampage through this idyll. Screams litter the evening sky, sounding like the high keys of a set of pianos.

He sayz, (in the low keys) 'Now look here a minute . . .' before I turn back, whack him right across the old kisser, whose sound reminds me of a hunk of dead, dense meat dropping to a stone tiled floor from a great height.

'OOH!' a woman cries, and puts her hand over her own mouth, as in empathy like. Must be his wife. Coupledom! But, you see, I recognized the man in an instant. Like I said, I'd only seen one of those Recovery Channels the once – he'd been, like, the expert sat at the head of a circle of alchies and addict types, nod-nodding his condescension. I flicked through once.

Just the once. *–A meetings per channel. Alcoholics Acknowledged meetings of squares and circles, asking those at home to listen to their experience, strength and hope. The irony. Flick the channel and come to Overeaters Acknowledged, where the latest victim, a big fatty, a skeletal skinny and a healthy ten 'group' secretary 'share' with each other. Hee haw. Hee haw.

Then there is one for Gamblers, Incest Survivors, Financial Anorexics, which had summat to do with not being turned on by cards of plastic and goldie-looking items and not being motivated enough by wage slavery in order to buy the things you are told you most definitely needed. There is also Gossips Acknowledged, Anger and Adrenaline Acknowledged, Sex Acknowledged (more than three times a week is considered too much), but yet, no Tabloid or Magazine of pointless picture barathrumics Acknowledged – anyhoo, 'tis all Acknowledged.

D'ya get me?

Me and Petra push him towards the BBQ, whose

tofu and Mediterranean roasted veg are sizzling away. The gaggle continue to stay together, for some reason, theyz do not grasp that it would be better for them to act solus, and run rings around us. But theyz know not. They claim the legacy of the language but know nought of ab esse ad posse. And now we are the only posse. In this garden anyway.

'Now. Now,' he sayz. The bass voice who had so bravely called out before is now hid behind the skirt of one of the 'fairer' sex. He he whore whore. I picks up the tofu tongs. Aluminium. Sleek. My front door is made of nothing more than old egg cartons. But the tofu is now burning. It reminds me of animadvertistine, ubicumque stes, fumum recta in faciem ferri? Everyone takes in a sharp intake of night air. I hold the tongs in the fire. And now I am determined to make a good impression! Georgia gets hold of him. Rolls up the sleeve of his checked shirt. He whimpers, but hardly moves, resigned to his fate. But I run by him, past one of the skirts and force it onto the face of the bass voice who had earlier instigated yet more suspicion, needful or otherwise. A howl goes up; shame the lunar was not full.

'OW! OW! OW!' he shouts, and runs around this

idyll. The women scream. Mid is somewhere else. She has found a tipple of wine, I see. A nasty red welt appears on the right side of his cheek – not unlike the scarlet letter. But this will end up, once the welt turns purple, into an 'I' – an 'I' for an 'I'; and I, in his case, is for Idiot, Imbecile, and Infuriating.

'Come. Grrrlz, it is time for us to be on our way,' I sayz.

'Now. Come on. I'm making a citizen's arrest,' one of them calls out. I laugh. HA! HA!

'How will you square this with your conscience?' this same non-descript woman asks.

'By looking at conscience as three syllables,' sayz I.

'But what about your Higher Power? What about . . .'

'Aah, the old H.P., how convenient,' sayz I. The fire in Georgia's eyes travels from her belly to her eyes. She lurches forward, so that her face almost meets the mad meddler's, and she screams in her face, 'I've got one H.P. Source missis, and that's *me* – only me can ever have my best interests, here,' she sayz, and holds her hand over her heart. Quite touching and all.

She does that now and again, does Georgia.

Very quiet and then WHAM! She'll explode with her deepest convictions.

It is a mark of the Grrrl.

And I love her the most because of it.

'Yeah!' I sayz backing her up.

Do they get us?

I doubt it.

Their type never would.

Never will. All they want is our peccavihs to make themselves feel better.

They don't got that fire. And they hate it.

Then we helps ourselves to a selection of exotic fruits – apples, pears, grapes, and then onto a selection of fine cheeses, apt for the area.

Hee hee. Haw haw.

Then I enters the back door and spy a bunch of car keys hanging on the kitchen wall. I go no further. Well, we've taken their idyll, theyz can keep their 'serenity'.

We leave their sweet ickle serenity, enters a side garage and zooms out in a very old, very ancient classic car. I do believe it is an old Morris Minor. Suits me, its paintjob matches the colour of our shoes and overalls. Khaki. But not our *La Perla*.

But then, no one would ever see those.

Only us.

Anyway, Georgia shouts in the car 'Everyday is like Sunday,' by our favourite old skooler, Morrissey, but, like, it just isn't 'appening, no voice control see. I put my foot right down but it isn't going too fast. Over an hour later we arrive back in the centre of Madchester.

3

We just manage to slip down behind Oxford Road, and park the car by old Little Ireland as a cop car speeds by. Sirens whirring. Talk about noise pollution.

We take a nice, calming walk by the old shitty canal, even though it is only supposed to be walked down now by the residents of the penthouses over-looking it.

Fucking hell! thinks I, stick a kiddies paddling pool in the middle of the M1 and build a shed and someone'd buy it for the view!

Mid has gone off into another one of her worlds again. I can tell. Georgia and Petra still have fire in their eyes. They are good Grrrlz. Theyz are my only 'hey sistaz, soul sistaz'. We walk slow back to Gutshot Rebos, all yawning away. We are still due at the compulsory youth day-centre tomorrow, aka

Tony Wilson Level 2 Community Centre, like all good Moss-Siders.

Pottery. Whose only aim is to keep us potty.

Fucking finger-painting.

Collages of tabloid pix. Antithesis to a Phrontistery.

It is enough to make you want to hang yourself.

Anyhoo . . . the old Gutshot Rebos is fuller than it was earlier in the evening. And what an evening! The meatheads have gone. Shame. Could have crowned the night off with a brawl.

A group of girlie wirlie Jordan wannabes are in the booth next to the one we usually have. And, by the looks of it, theyz are on the wheatgrass with Phrontistery drops added. Which we most certainly no way never needed. One of them, a plastic blond, is yapping away ten to the dozen. 'YeahandthenI wannadoaninstallationartpiece, Whitwortharedeffo interestedandallthat, and . . . then . . . Iwantoneof thosemakeupcontracts,andthengetanactingpartonyo oftvI'mdeadtalentedme, rightcontenderforlivingthe DREAMI'M-A-STAR-YEAH!' and she starts to giggle.

You can tell she isn't used to the Phrontistery

drops in the old wheatgrass. She won't just have verbal diarrhoea later on.

Hee hee haw haw.

The meatheads would have loved her scratch on their goldie looking episemons. I look over to the bar and there, perched on stools, is a bunch of Blyton-esques from Granada Studios. Execs, actors, LIVINGTHEDREAM! Whatthefuckever!

Then I look over at the blonde with verbal diarrhea, and she keeps on glancing sideways at them. Impression management. Theyz all fucking at it. I want to stand on one of the tables and shout 'YOU LOT, BLONDIE HERE WANTS TO BE DISCOVERED!' And on any other night I wouldn't have hesitated. But I am yawning a bit too much now. One wheatgrass minus and then I'll be off.

We take our regular booth, sit and observe. Comfortable in our own silence. Our own unspoken connections that could only be ruined by the impression management of smalltalk. And then, my ears widen a little more, and they zone in on one of the voices at the bar – the smelly Granada lot. One of the old men, and he is old, he'd have to be, well, he's talking about:

'Opposites. As within, so without, versus As without,

so within. Nature versus nature. Men versus women. Masculinity versus femininity. Sobriety versus drunkenness. Skaz versus skez.'

He just reels them off. They give a few nods of the old head and a few Blyton-esque piano sounding laughs and make to leave.

And, my dear sistaz, if I'm being truly honest, I has to admit, I want to be wivv 'em.

I want those conversations.

Those nods of the head.

But not the fucking Blyton-esque hee heeing. That, yeah, is a total no-go.

It is more like wanting to be saved by Edward Bond.

Hello sadness, sayz I, (to meself) and sadness waves back, not drowning, just waving.

But Mid, as if reminded of her former life, sneers, 'Oh DO shut the fuck up!' from the corner of her mouth as they leave.

I feel the sadness disappear and I sayz hello to the fire.

'Bitch! Stupid tired boring little MID!'

I can tell she is hurt. Her eyes glaze over with a film of tears. She thought it is what I had also wanted to say after them, I gather. I nudge her.

'OW!' she whines.

'Ow?' sayz I.

'We'z all tired now, innit,' sayz Petra, trying to placate.

'Innit,' sayz Georgia. 'You've been funny peculiar all the evening long though Mid, sort it out,' sayz Petra.

We gets outside and begins the forty minute walk back to Moss-Side.

Mid walks ahead with Georgia.

Petra walks beside me.

'Listen right, Alex, you know I love you and all that, we'z sistaz, but listen, yeah, you has to lay off Mid, you're gonna push her away from us and all that. If it was me or Georgia there'd be payback, d'ya get me?' she sayz.

I can feel the old flame reaching up into me chest. And I go in for impression management.

'Listen Petra, lah, there has to be a leader, and I'm *it*, always have been. I'm not talking about leader of who you are and 'owt like that, but in terms of Group Purpose, it's important –'

I trail off.

I am hit by the sadness again. It is now shouting,

'OI, I'M HERE, LISTEN TO ME,' now drowning, not waving.

Hello again, sayz I (to meself).

'What? What's important?' Petra asks.

'Just forgeddaboudit,' sayz I.

'Everyone's knackered,' she concludes.

'You understand though Petra, what that oldie is saying, it's important – to me, you know?' I ask, and, for a second I panic (inside) and thinks, oh no, what if I've been like, deluding myself for all these years that Petra and Georgia 'get me', but they really haven't?

'I know Alex, I know, you're barathrumic, you need something more – even than us, we've always known that.'

As soon as she said the first three words the tone didn't match the meaning. It is as if she is saying to the world I KNOW ALEX, instead of I *know*, Alex.

But it isn't the words that told me she 'knew', it is, like, telepathic, or psychic or whatever it is. And then, like, I begin to think about the oldies before the birth of words themselves, when the picture ruled supreme. How did they communicate with each other? Theyz didn't go round with a stick, hoping there'd be a smooth enough bit of sand or earth to draw a symbol, did they? So, what is it? Is it head to head? Telepathy? Mustabeen.

But then my heart sinks into the pit of me stummick.

What if those who did nothing but watch Recovery Hour, work from home and stare at tabloid pictures are 'right', or whatever?

What if they are righter than us? Of me? D'ya get me?

Or that they are purer? Or the world had regressed, not progressed, and we are back to pre-scholastic days? What if regression is progression?

What then?

What of the future.

SHUT UP, I sayz (to meself).

But then, just as I am about to relax within myself and gear up for a night of rest we come across Milly Molly Bandy and her sidekicks – who, actualie, couldn't kick sideways for love, nor money. Although they'd give it a damn good try for the latter, but wouldn't care a fig for the former.

Now, Milly Molly Bandy makes me sick to my stummick, she has her plastic tits hanging out, or *up!* And she has her hands on her well fed, only too fertile hips.

She stops and raises her hand behind her, to signal to her girlie curlie wurlies to fall in line behind.

We stop in a line, not single file,

        but across – we are a team.

'Yeah, where'ya goin' then?' Milly Molly Bandy asks, chewing her gum like some sad, mad and dated old fucking cliché from an old gang film.

'Tits not dropped through sheer weight yet then?' Petra asks. Petra can not stand her, nor can any of us. Mid giggles. Nerves. She was once one of Milly's girlies wirlies, and we don't usu-alie poach and all that stuff, you see, you're in one camp or another for a reason. You are a Grrrl because you stand by a certain set of principles, ethos, laden with a liberal dose of anger, or Etna, which is a fully acknowledged and embraced part of who you are. But we rescued Mid.

Mid had wanted to be rescued.

We had got Mid to get in touch with her inner Angria child.

'Some old meatheads are looking to add to their goldie looking episemons in Gutshot Rebos, don't ya wanna run down there?' I asks, with a sneer.

'Don't do goldie looking badges,' she sayz, in a ner ner ner ner ner voice.

'In fact,' she continues, (she's feeling daring tonite I sphinx), 'looks like you and your lot don't do anything goldie looking.'

I'm now thinking, is this s'posed to be an insult. Poor Cow! No idea what she's talking about. We laugh.

She pulls a face. Her own, thankfully. She takes a strand of her hair and twiddles with it, still chewing her gum.

I will the two to meet – hair and gum. That, dear sistaz, would be a funny shot for her to play back in the old archive of impressions management that she no doubt plays back every night before she goes to beddy bye byes, to see what moves and gestures she could fine tune for the next day.

PAFFETIK.

'Your old muvvaz still sat in the old Duchess of New York then?' Milly Molly Bandy asks.

I look to each of my Grrrlz. We shake our heads, as if to say, PAFFETIK.

'At least we, unlike you and your lot, will not fall prey to our muvvaz histories, now will we?' sayz I.

'Eh?' she asks. You see, there's no fucking point in us having them as our so called rivals, it's like saying Queen Madge had a rival in the form of a Big Brother contestant.

PAFFETIK.

But we couldn't be picky, there are no other rivals for us in Moss-Side. Most of 'em had taken their muvvaz route – even Milly Molly Bandy and her girls had, but then . . . They had insufficiently formed/exercised Phrontisteries.

'Do you know somefin Milly,' sayz I, 'Beauty hides behind the scenes of the May Day parade. If we want to find it, we must demolish the scenery.'

'You're gonna demolish us, are yuz? Like to see you bloody well try, wouldn't we girls?'

The girls look nervous. Well, I may have been projecting, but they should do as well.

'You see, you don't even get the gist, the GIST of what we say, do you?' I sayz.

'You callin' me stupid?' she asks. PAFFETIK.

'Yes! Stupid!' Mid pipes up.

Like a cat on the old tin roof type thingie Milly Girl springs into the air and goes to do the old Cantona Kung Fuey to poor Mid. Well, she can't let go of the grudge of the poached. Mid jumps back and holds up her hands, also in Kung Fuey style. Don't know what it is about the old martial arts but theyz really having their showcase today.

'Go on then Mid, show her what you always wanted way back when,' sayz I.

'Yeah, go on, give it her,' shouts Petra.

'Go for it Mid,' Gergia shouts.

Milly Molly Bandy takes a step back and reaches for her long goldie looking chain belt and begins swinging it round, like a lighthouse signal for kerb-crawlers. She is giving too much of her true nature away.

Hee hee whore whore.

Then the old sirens appear; whirring in the distance. Like Dickensian rogues we 'scarper', we do. That is, we get into single file and jump, no, leap, more graceful than the lead dancer of the Nutcracker, for we are little nutcrackers, over their pretty little itsy-bitsy heads. From where we get our energy I do not know. But it is a requirement for Grrrlz. Always yare!

We come to the field off of Great Western Street, where Georgia and her family live. Theyz travellers. Some call them gippos, pikies, tinkers, knackers, which is like calling a black a nigger. But it is still deemed A O.K., even after all this time. But Georgia is defiant. That's why I like her. From the minute I knew I was 'different' there she had been – trying to keep her head held high, not only for herself, but on behalf of her family, an entire tribe, and thus for everyone who wanted something different, or who had found themselves in a different world – in a world that only grudgingly allowed their old caravans and gas bottles, lest theyz go round burning their houses down.

Which we Grrrlz did anyway.

Hee hee. Haw haw.

'Nightey nightey to you and yours then,' sayz I.

Me, Petra and Mid continue round the field and through the estate. I come to the block I have lived in since the day I had been born. It is Moss-Side Block 2, between Burgess and Royce Way. Mid is in Block 4 and Petra in Block 5. I get into the main piss-stinking lobby and, as per usual, a few of the residents have failed to make their way up to their front doors and so have collapsed from drugs, drink, (or sugar, hee hee haw haw) or just collapsed from the unbearable heaviness of being and can not, for the moment, get up.

'It's all too fuckin' pointless, innit,' an old woman shouts up to me.

'FUCK OFF!' I shouts back.

Belligerency is Queen.

I enter our abode and there, as per usual, on the second hand sofa, lies me mum.

Too many stouts.

Old Trout!

I enter the box of a kitchen.

Nowt there.

Good job I had a little feast of fruit and fine cheeses in Cheshire! I tut tut and go into the bathroom where I wish I could have a nice long soak, but we on the estates we are only allowed a quota of water (hot and cold) per day, which usually meant either a half bath OR shower in the morning. I brush my teeth and spit out the dental foam onto the porcelain, imagining that it is life itself, yeah.

I seek solace in my box room where lies my single bed. I take a deep breath. I pull the canvas rug up off the floor and then prise up one of the old rotten floorboards and there, my dear sistaz, is my stash of mind power – that is, BOOKS! I is in the fullness of haecceity now, my dear sistaz.

I pull out old Nietzsche and pick out only the

sweetest ripest cherries from the variourum filled pages:

> *The great periods of our life occur when we gain the courage to rechristen what is bad about us as what is best.*

I ponder this, which is no doubt widdershins to the majority, as I had pondered it many an evening before. It still has the power to churn my stummick over a million times.

Well, not quite. But you get the drift.

I am tired, my dear sistaz, and, what wiv the strife with Mid, a tad emotional, and now a droplet of salt water – just another part of the body's chemistry launched into play by this emotion laden thought, that in turn had been built and developed by the hands of emotion herself through surrounding systems, runs down my pale face.

And yet, the fire in me belly, oh loyal Etna of wronged goddesses that has ever existed, both in myth and other worlds, doesn't let me down. It will, I hope, be a flame ready to soar to the heights of the cause for as long as I live.

It has taken a long time for me to be able to see

through the bullshit and rechristen my belligerency borne from longing as a good thing.

Good for me.

A reminder I most certainly need.

Knowledge would only have a slight allure if there weren't so much shame to overcome in achieving it. Too true, my dear sistaz, only too true.

And then, book on my pillow beside me, I fall sound asleep.

4

I wake up. It is eight – that dreaded hour, but widdershins of the official Recovery Hour. I am still knackered. I do not jest when I say that the thought of going to the Tony Wilson Level 2 community centre makes me want to throw myself off the top of Moss-Side Block 2.

But that has been done many times before.

No one bats an eyelid.

Less a statement, more a gift.

To 'Them'.

But I'm not going to do it their way entirely. I never do.

I am unable to. Poor Tony Tone. Blasphemy of his name and intentions.

I put the book from last nite underneath the old rickety floorboards. Then I leave my box room and bang on me muvva's door where she's no doubt crawled into, alabandical, in the middle of the night after pissing up the old stinky sofa.

It is, my dear sistaz, like living with an errant animal. But the behaviour is just a symptom of . . . I hear you think, dear readerz. Yes, but you *can't* let the bastards grind you down.

Can you?

A man called Mandela once said that when he was imprisoned he told his fellow prisoners to give up smoking. Being locked away is a loss of freedom, but being beholden to the old cancer sticks and *then* to the guards with the keys, well, that is *another* loss of freedom. And it is bad enough being a prisoner one time over, never mind 'owt else. And so they did. And they were locked up for twenty-seven years.

And they stayed healthy.

Both in mind and body. Coz they gave up smoking at the start.

See, I'm not all bad. I like sharing those little senti-mental snippets wiv u.

Anyhoo . . . I bang on me muvvafukka's door.

'WAKE UP' I yell at the top of me voice.

'FUCK OFF' she shouts, 'BAD HEAD.'

'BAD FUCKIN' MUVVA,' I shoot back.

Well, the old bitch might have returned alabandical as always, and pissed up the sofa, but I
am gonna make it hard for her to get clean. And
so I have my share of water plus hers which made
almost a full bath. Hot soapy suds.

And I lie there, like that, and fall asleep. zzzzzz
zzzzz.

I even have a dream.

About Mid it is.

I dreams that she has been allowed out of the
day centre and is sent back to the old Blyton school
from where she once came, and she is sneering and
laughing all over her stupid face at me, in blazer
and tie and all that, glass of wine in hand.

I wake up at nine. Just as the day at the Level 2
Community Centre is beginning. Or half an hour
after the Blyton's school start their first lesson –
philosophy. *Let no one ignorant of geometry enter!*

Followed by English literature.

Leavis-led and prescribed.

Followed by mathematics.

No grey areas.

And I, with my Phrontistery, will get to do what
I'm made to do every other fucking day – finger-
paint, photo-collages, 'life skills', which basically

meanz learning how to fill out a digi-application for a future job, and memorizing the Recovery Channel numbers. 71 for AA, 45 for NA etcetera, etcetera, etcetera.

They know I can read. But we don't talk about that – because half of the Centre supervisors can't.

Anyhoo . . . I thinks I will just lounge around in my dressing gown and *La Perla*. But then, wouldn't you know it, the doorbell buzzes the life out of me.

'FUCK OFF' I shoutz.

It rings again.

I gets up and bangs on muvva's door.

'FUCK OFF,' she shoutz.

'You're always tellin' me it's *your* door!' sayz I.

But it is futile. I answer the fucking fucked up pain in the arse door.

'Yes?' sayz I.

'DAY CENTRE.'

That's all. And the uniformed official dashes off to another door to issue another 'reminder'. I slam the door.

'Watch the door!' muvva shouts.

What can I do?

I put on my day centre uniform – grey trousers, grey baseball boot type things and grey cheap sweat-shirt type thingie.

We are grey.

What more can I say?

The Blytons, though, they have the whole kit and caboodle. Royal blue and gold tie. Badge on the blazer. Satchels. Enchiridions.

We just have to make ourselves grey and get ourselves there.

I smooth my hair back, splash cold water on my face, and leave the block. Some oldie destructives from the evening before are still in the foyer. Could be dead or alive. If it starts stinking worse than usual then we'll find out. The day is grey. Which, actually, unlike my centre 'uniform' I don't mind. Grey days can perk me up, provide a blank canvas against which I can connect with my emotional barometer. Yes, I do take note, and acknowledge at regular times throughout the day. And why not? No one else asks me how I am. So I ask myself. Alex, how are thee? I walk through the estate. And what a state! From here I can see Georgia's mumsie, fag in gob, lugging around an old gas canister, god only knows where they still get them! But at least, for now, it ensures their self-sufficiency, or near as. Her hacking cough barks through the air. A few dogs follow her, desperate for their brekkie. I wish I had a dog. Or a cat. But I have my secret enchiridions. And the power they give my Phrontistery. It is my pet. My power. I walk around the old pit, with its carpet of shattered windscreens, and regular glitterings of squares of foil, and the promise they have maybe delivered to their loser users. I think, briefly, of the pix-collaging that will, at this very minute, be taking place at the Tony Wilson Level 2 Community Centre. One of the supervisors will be wondering, if at all, where Alex is. Alex is strolling. Wondering. Wandering. I walk toward the centre, alas. But, instead of going up Broadfield Road, I turn left, up Great Western Street. There is an old café off of Keswick Street. It is called Alvino's. There is the odd bout of trouble here, but not too much in the daytime. I spy a 'newspaper' underneath one of the tables and so that determines at which I take my seat. I lean under and pull it out. It is today's date.

So, I has a cup of coffee brought over and leisurely sip sip sip it, valuing myself as the philosopher that I am. That is, lover of knowledge. There is no other brekkie. One has gotten used to it since young, what wiv havin' an alchie-holic muvvafukka.

And, my dear sistaz:

Why is she an alchie-holic muvvafukka?

And why should alchie-holic muvvafukkas be allowed to bring new life into this world?

This 'newspaper' has its usual pix of smilin' hand-shaking official types, and plastic implanted women stickin' everythin' out.

The same old, same old.

Now, what I would like to see, dear sistaz, is headlines that create debate, tackle issues from *every* perspective.

And what do we get?

Pictures.

Like we are some two year old Blyton types. And then there are, on the same page, pictures of Moss-Side alleyways with oneword headlines shouting **DISGUSTING!**

And **YOBS!** And, get this for oxymoronic: yob 'culture'.

And then, on the opposite side of the same page, news of footballers' wage rises. Some things never change, eh? But then, in the middle of this paper, the biggest selling in the land, is a centre page spread on **MOSS-SIDE TROUBLES** – what they mean is, not like Moss-Side *has* troubles, but that Moss-Side troubles *THEM*.

Hee hee haw haw.

I take another deep slurp of my coffee and read the bold print words made up of two syllables or less. But, my dear sistaz, it boils down to one fing, and one fing only – parental discipline. These yoof, they sayz, have not been disciples of their parents. Well, I sphinx, halle-loojah! And thank the H.P. for that!! But then it is back to the unavoidable ongoing debate in me head – Freud versus . . . But then the articles goes on, and, forever wanting to coin a new phrase or strapline it sayz:

'ANGRY YOUNG WOMEN'

Well, I concludes, theyz aren't rong on that, so theyz aren't.

THE ANGRY YOUNG MEN HAD FAILED. SOULED OUT.

And theyz hardly mentioned their female counterparts anyway. Sillitoe, Barstow, Braine – and Osborne?! Forget it – Blyton-eezy!

But then it reminds me of an article I'd read

once from a journal I'd kind of 'borrowed' from some Blyton's house that I'd let meself into. The gist is this: maybe we, that is, Troubled and Troublesome Yoof, would be better off, that is, become more Blytonesie and manageable, if we could be encouraged to be more cultured, and that. I had laughed me head off. Parts of my life have become art itself, but they, the gatekeepers of culture *wouldn't*, or *couldn't* recognize that. Then, like, there is, in this journal, the counterargument. It is one of those journals that wants to portray a 'balanced' set of opinions and wants to be 'polite', or present themselves as such. It sayz, 'Nonsense!' Byron was a right fucking fucked up bastard, innit!

I love that. I drop a few tokens for my coffee and leave. It is time, my dear sistaz, for a day at the centre. I will show you just how paffetik it is.

I pass by the rusting old railings and enter the descrted courtyard. The building looms over me; a Victorian building it is. Not many of them around no more, for sure. It still has old oil radiators. At least we don't have no nuclear power. I walk down the long, forbidding corridor that smells of plasticine and cabbage. Voices of dissent echo around the building. Fuck offs are aplenty, and the occasional THUDS of things lobbed around. Doors slammed. The odd cry. The odd scream. It would, I feel, be odder if there weren't the odd cry/scream. It's odd there aren't more. I enter room 7.A. Georgia is sat at the grey table, her head in her arms. She looks up, smiles sleepily, then puts her head back down. This supervisor is yet another irregular. I have not seen her before, that is. But she will, no doubt, be worthy of the vilipend treatment. They all are, in some way. Petra is flicking paint from a thick brush against a wall. It is, however, a wall set aside for such endeavours. It means nish. It gets white-washed every evening. This feeble, fucking futile attempt at a pocket of self-expression. Widdershins and mumpsimus, my dear sistaz, sheer widdershins and mumpsimus. There is, however, no Mid. I wonder. I sit down and pick at my nails. Nowt doing.

'You Alex?' the supervisor asks.

I look at her. I nod.

'Go to the manager's office straightaway,' she sayz, continuing to stroll around the room, as though she's a lady of yore out on the circuit in some Bath spa in Austen-era.

'Why?'

'How would I know?' she asks.

I grunt, and scrape the chair from the table. I

strut to the manager's office. Outside the manager's office is a tempered glass kiosk. The gatekeeper.

'Go straight in,' she sayz and continues tapping away at a keyboard.

I enter without knocking. She, the manager, is watering plants. Plenty of them, all around her office. She is truly privileged to have so much oxygen being produced for her in one small space. I close the door and there sits a bitch of all bitches.

It is Tilda Lawsondottir.

'Why are you late?' manager asks.

'I was up most of the night with muvva,' I repliez.

'I ask why you were late, not how you spent your night,' manager sayz. I want to rub her face in the muddiest of mud now.

'I got hardly any sleep, and thus, dear miss, slept in and, it should be noted, am still k-nackered.'

'Self-pity won't ish, life's unfair, get used to it!' sayz she.

'Well ma'am, thank you for those words of wisdom, now that you've said them my mind has become, like, totally transformed, it's a miracle. NOT!' sayz I.

Tilda Lawsondottir butts in now, stands up from her comfy seat and circles me.

'Think you're funny, don'tcha? By the way, where

were you and your little grislies last night?' she asks, her hands on her hips like a prison warder.

'I don't got no grislies – you mean us Grrrlz?'

'Whatever!' she replies, like some petulant American yoof from way back when and whose second favourite saying is 'Talk to the hand!'

Stupid Kunt.

'Well, before I had to be home to look after muvva we went out for a nice saunter, through our city's finest steets, innit.'

'What 'finest' streets? You're being shady again!' she sayz.

'Shady? Don't you mean snide? Snidey? SHADY?'

'Answer the question!'

'Down Upper Lloyd Street, into town, is it allowed oh authoritative one?'

'Four girls dressed like mechanics were seen stealing a car – minimum prison term for Moss-Siders is two years.

'NOWT! I know three other girls, as I'm sure most other girlies do, but that meanz what? Besides, four mechanics? Well it's not unusual to see them around cars! D'ya get me?' sayz I.

'I can't see many people getting you, do YOU GET ME?' she shouts, right by my ear now, rood bitchy-face.

Now, my dearest sistaz, here is a woman who knows zilch about relativism. Or Nietzsche's Perspectivism. That is, she isn't even only seeing fings from her own POV, but that of the Acknowledged State.

It has one perspective.

The room can only be seen from their own angle, even though they are all for panopticons.

Innit! To get into our heads one needs to speak the lingo – walk the balletic walk – get into the whole method fingy, *d'ya get me, lah*?

They don't.

They always liked to think theyz do.

Hee hee haw haw.

What it is, is this, right, there's someone with blazin' eyes in the dusty corner where the rubbish is kept, and there's these dandies in the main part of the room. And they keep poking the blazin' eye person in the corner – with a stick – coz they is too scared to get up close and personal, *d'ya get me*?

Instead of gettin' in the corner and standin' next

to her – sharing the view and then seeing all the more clearly their own role in our shared existenz.

But their troof is *their* troof and we apparently don't know the meanin' of the word, cos we don't have *theirs*.

The fucked up fuckin' Blytonesie still sphinx their troof is THE troof.

Like their history.

Like their future.

I've got me own. And in this economy, it's derided and shat upon, my dearest sistaz.

'Right, chop chop, back to class!' she orders, now breakin' into my glorious forts.

Fucking Bitch!

With my fakest of fake personas – which still falls woefully short of the one that is allied to their troof and perspective and all that, I smile. My flame is behaving like it has just had a liberal dose of alchie-hol poured on it – baited. I hold my breath for a good few secs in order to deprive my dearest flame of provocative oxygen for a little while. Coz, you know, I could, quite easily, strangle them both with my barest of hands and then frow them both over Moss-Side Block 2 – not just cos theyz spineless bitches with no perspectives of their own or 'owt like that, but coz theyz dissed me too much. And to bait and diss someone already in the corner – well, it just gets to be too much.

D'ya get me?

Anyhoo . . . Tilda starts beep beeping.

The voice of her controller breaks into the room and calls her off, like the robot that she is.

'Right You!' sayz she.

'Yes?' sayz I, in my prettiest Blyton-esque voice. There is nothing guaranteed to wind those Blyton types up more than the mockery of their own voices.

'Now listen, cheeky madam! You just get back to class, THIS INSTANT – I have to go and deal with yet another of your lot over in Moss-Side Block – anyway, get going and, madam, **remember one thing** – you are being watched very closely indeed. What happened last night, well, count your hours of freedom, that's all I'll say! You've got a roof over your head, food in your belly, you should be grateful!' sayz she. 'Count your hours of freedom . . . you should be grateful, too many people looking into the causes of you Moss-Siders' disaffection and so-called alienation,' her voice replays itself in me head as I walk back down the corridor to 'class'.

The irony.

Hee hee haw haw.

I do spend a minute or so tho', weighing up her words of wisdom and I reach this conclusion:

She could go fuck herself.

If I get caught for last night, or even for how I plan to expel and express my anger this evening, well, that is a hazard of being the authentic self that I am, innit. I am not in dear old Blyton, so I can't behave like the good little girl they want me to be – and it wouldn't get me anywhere I want to be anyway. It is too Sisyphean. All this head-scratching and omphaloskepsis – it makes me laff me glorious head right off me shoulders, it does. Why are they not head-scratching on the causes of what makes themselves, the Blytons, and then work from there, eh? Why not work out their own role instead of constantly looking to us? 'Badness' is of the self, but self is of the society, the structures, the systems, the programming, *innit?* And so it has to be vented against those who initiate and conform to those rules.

Or.

Is it that just bad people are punished for doing somefink really bad in a former life and so are sent to the man god to be born into Moss-Side Block whatever?

Nature or nurture.

Nature or culture?

I have fort and fought about it for a few years now, dear sistaz, and, what comes to me now is this:

fuck it all and sit self-expression on the throne and bow down to her and carry out her wishes. Turn the anger OUTWARDS, not INWARDS.

Coz, you see, inwards meanz you are creating more problems for yourself, on behalf of THEM, whereas OUTWARDS meanz you're creating problems for THEM, where it belongs. Where it longs to be. Depression or expression? Which is it to be, my dear sistaz? Which?

Aah, the old sophy of Philo always bestows its glacier-like clarity to perk me up, yet provokes the old flame into a pure belly fire that is the mark of my place in the city of authenti.

It makes me feel like Lady of me own Manor and all that. And then, there and then, halfway down this Victorian corridor that stinks of plasticine, cabbage, and hypocrisy, I decide I will not return to class, no, instead I will spend some time on my own education. I will pay a visit to the old book trader in the blue light district on Tib Street in what is the So-no of Madchester. And no, I won't even bother returning home; I will keep on my greyest of grey attire, for I am feeling dangerous.

If THEY want to pick me up and force me back then they can – but whilst I am *living* MY life. I am a political prisoner. Yare.

I stroll along Tib Street with a whistle. I check my emotional weather and ask myself how I am. And I feel myself cheery up a bit more when I stand outside the blackened shop front of the nameless little book traders which, on the outside, bears the façade of a discount crockery store. I enter. Gerald, a man in his seventies, sits behind his little battered and beaten up old counter. His eyes brighten once theyz see me.

He thinks I am a 'breath of fresh air.' Me and my learning. His little auto-didact.

I agree.

'How are you Alex dear?' he asks.

'I'm fine thank-you Gerald, and thou?'

'Mustn't grumble, mustn't grumble, not exactly a rip-roaring trade in plates though, eh?'

We both laugh. Ha ha ha ha!

'What today then Alex dear?' he asks.

I think he's a breath of fresh air too.

Which is also at a premium in old Madchester.

'De Beauvoir?' he asks.

The flame rises.

'NO! NOT THE SARTREAN PIMPETTE FAKE AUTHENTIC!' sayz I. Although I know my labeling of her is a tad extreme, 'tisn't far from the mark.

'No. No, not De Beauvoir then. How about Lessing?'

'Mmmmm, Lessing, perhaps.'

'Aphra Behn?'

'Mmm, maybe,' sayz I, but I know almost all of her words off by heart. The one thing that can be said about those of the late seventeenth and early eighteenth century is this. Those few women were far more radical than their sisters of the next century, which goes to show how the notion of progression, and linearity, is redundant.

'Or Wollstonecraft?'

I part with some pieces of paper for old Wooly Wollstonecraft. Well what could I do? I bid goodbye to dear old Gerald-o and leave ye oldie shoppe, the book underneath my grey jumper. I take a few less public shortcuts, not wanting to parade myself walking through the old Piccashitty Gardens.

I hear a whistle behind me.

I continues to walk.

I hear it again, and it's aimed at me.

The flame rises a little.

I am ready to fight.

Another whistle.

I spin around.

My dear sistaz, who is it I hear you ask, you're dying to know.

Two suited and booted men. Ten years or so older than I. Oh, what a day this is turning out to be. Anticipation is in the air once again. They smile that half sneering, slimey smile they sphinx cannot be detected by anyone other than those men in their secret sneering club. One of them reaches right inside his long coat, pulls out a wallet and takes out a few crisp notes.

I laffs to myself, sistaz. They have recognized my

day centre uniform that signifies Moss-Side and
lack of . . . everything. They, on the other hand,
are of an upper-Blyton-esque cut. They remind me
of old Chaz Dickens on his walks round London
and his 'chit-chats' with the girls of the night. That's
the image that comes to mind. Another idea hit
me.

'Yes?' sayz I, and I widen my eyes as far as I can
and raise my voice as much as I can. I even make
myself blush. A la vulnerable.

D'ya get me, lah?

'So, then, little girlie,' sayz the blondie looking
one. 'Would you like us to take you out for a nice
fancy schmancy dinner?'

'A fancy schmancy dinner? For mio mio?' sayz
I, my eyes still wide.

'Yes, for *YOU*!' sayz the browney haired one.

'We thinks you are special,' he sayz.

'Mio mio? Special?' sayz I.

'Yes, you've never been Discovered before, have
you?' sayz the blonde.

'Discovered? No. Never.' Sayz I.

'Well, let's go to dinner – and talk about . . .
YOU!' sayz blondie.

'Mio? My-o!' They led the way to Dean's – which

they term 'fancy schmancy', and which I know only to be very very mediocre.

They keep looking at my face – which I have to exercise into pleased, surprised, humble, unworthy, girlie – all at the same time.

I am having SUCH fun fun fun!

The waitress brings over our menus.

'Now, Lexie,' sayz they, *for that's the name I gave them – seems more appropriate and all that,*

'Now, you can choose ANYTHING you want,' sayz the brownie haired one.

'ANYTHING?!' sayz I.

'Anything at all!' sayz blondie.

'WOW!' replies me. And so I has the steak, well done, cos I am a girlie and all that – even though I would usually have gone for blue or rare, but that's only when me and the Grrrlz get it t'gevva.

D'ya get me?

I'm sure you do.

He whore, he whore.

Then, after we munch munch munch, my stomach feels like a lead disposal unit and I know a bit of a workout is most definitely needed.

'So then, now that we've done a bit of chitchatting, what say you come up to our Grand Hotel room?' sayz blondie.

'Ooh, Grand Hotel and all that too?'

'Yes,' sayz brownie haired one.

'Ooh, well, I'm not sure . . .' sayz I, picking at the corner of my peasant fed mouth with me little finger.

'You'll be safe with us!' sayz blondie.

'Safe? Yes!' sayz I, and follow them into Grand Hotel Number 1. Their room is indeed big and grand, in a heavy oak burdensome kind of way.

'So, little girl,' sayz they, falling into the roles of their sickoscripto.

'What games would you like to play?' they sayz.

'Mmm, well, there is this game that I like,' sayz I.

'But first, would little girl like a drinkie winkie?' sayz blondie.

'Mmm, I'm not old enough to drinkie winkie, and so I won't,' sayz I. But I watch as they pour themselves big greedy gulpies. I wonder when theyz going to dull their senses even more despite the nepenthe quality of these desired games. But play *my* game first I will.

Sometimes, my dear sistaz, the ends is more important than the means. The Journey is primo, but sometimes the stops along the way aren't worth missing a blink for, so I shall spare you. Ten minutes have passed and theyz now both tied up in their birthday suits.

One to the big Grand bed, and the other to a chair.

Hee hee haw haw.

I slip out one of their big leather belts from their troosers.

And WHACK! WHACK! I go.

And scream like girlie wirlies they do. And now welts appear not unlike the tong-inflicted burn on bass-voice of Cheshire. Theyz now prisoners of the imbroglio they had wanted to inflict upon me.

With their welted bodies screaming for relief, I leave them, still tied.

And, my sistaz, I take a leisurely stroll home, my stomach no longer feeling like lead, but as light as a Blyton promise.

I arrive back to Moss-Side Block 2. Muvvafukka has woken and is having first drink of the day

- getting ready for the evening so she can resume her drinkie winkies with the other muvvafukkaz.

'Where'vya bin?' she utters.

'Mind your own fuckin' biz,' sayz I. There is no risk of antipelargy here.

'Ooh charmin' how you speak to your muvva!' she sayz.

'Yes, charming!' sayz I. I remove the Wollstonecraft enchiridion and make it safe. Then I return to the 'living' room and make sure the seat of the settee is dry and slump in it, my feet throbbing slightly from all the tramping I have done during the day. It is half an hour before CRH – the Compulsory Recovery Hour. Muvva is sat in the kitchen, twiddlin' her grey hair. The box is left to blair, on and on, anon. It is halfway through some pre-recovery blah. The might of King Anon. An on an' on an' on.

I skwitch it off right there, lest I put me foot in through the box's face.

'Yer s'posed to leave that on, they can tell you know,' she warns, and takes another sip of her concrete dew or brutalist brew, or whatever it is called.

'So why don't YOU watch it then?' sayz I.

'Coz I choose not to – I choose to make my life easier by drownin' me sorrows,' sayz she.

'I have a much more organic nepenthe',' sayz I.

'Yeah yeah! D'ya know how ridiculous you sound coming out with that language?' she asks.

'Yeah. Fuck off!' I repliez.

'Where are you off to now? You know, you're gonna get into so much trouble my girl, out there, whatever trouble it is you're creating.'

'Creating, yes, trouble, not for us mommy dearest,' sayz I, with a glint in me eye. I cannot abide her company. I quickly change out of my grey attire.

In my *La Perla* (peach) and my overalls and balletic pumps I slide down the scratched banisters of Moss-Side Block 2. There, at the bottom, in the pissy lobby are the three Grrrlz.

Waiting for their leader.

'Here she is, our leader,' sayz Mid.

I do wish she wouldn't be so Blytonesie obsee-kweeus. It can be very grating and, as I'm now sure I don't have to spell out – the height of inauthentik.

'You're a bit late this even,' sayz Petra.

'Late? A bit, yes,' sayz I. 'I had a bit of unexpected play today, dearest grrrlz, which I shall tell you all about later ons, when we getz a bit bored, perhaps.'

'Tired still?' asks Georgia. 'Tired no more, yare and up and at it dear Georgia, yare and up and at it – how's all at the caravan site?' asks I.

'Noisy, angria and angria,' sayz she.

'All good then,' sayz I.

'Yes, angria and angria, all good,' sayz Petra, with a bit of an unappealing grinnie across her facey.

'Am I missing summat? Oh, I geddit, ok, no more angria against Mid then? Is that it?' I asks.

They three kind of half nod – indecision, I dunno.

'Mid, you are middling mid alright, and always will be, I s'pose. We'll have to make do, but no more angria against each other, unless . . . nothing, is that clear?' asks I in the spirit of hand holding demo of crassy.

'Aye aye!' sayz Mid in that stupid cheesy am dram way, willing her not to follow with 'Kap Tin!' for that would, I'm positive, have rendered contract of no angria towards each other null and void.

'Yes,' sayz Petra, 'no more angria towards each other – Mid is just as much a person as we,' she adds.

'Ok, ok, she is just as much a person as we are, is that what you want to hear?' sayz I, the flame now reaching higher and higher.

'This is good, talking, comm-uni-skating and all that, listenin' to each other, as eekwals,' sayz she.

'Eekwals?' sayz I.

'Yes, and, talkin' bout eekwollity, and all that, Wella the Irish sayz we could, like, professionalize our endeavours, our outward angria – demos and police and state take on, and all that, good, yes?' sayz she.

Georgia raises her eyebrows at me and then looks down at her ballet shoes. Skeptissism writ large across her facey. Her people had tried the official.

And died offalish defs.

'Professionlize? I don't care much for this, and I suppose that by listening to a right on democrassy lover who's also an ex-middy like Mid here can just come in and organize us in her Blytonesie ways?' sayz I.

Mid looks down at her shoes now.

Petra pleads with her eyes.

'OK then, as you wish. How can I stop you on your paths into the city of authenti?' sayz I, with a shrug of me shoulders.

Mid looks up, with tears in her eyes, as if to say pseudo-Blytonesie democrassy has won the day, the ethics and arseaches of Blyton, her gods, have been right and ultimate trooful after all.

Aaah!

There is no 'elpin' some people at all, because they could never get beyond their inner evangelical missionary.

'Good-o, now, hows about a strolley wollie down to the old Gutshot Rebos?' sayz Petra.

'You read my own foughts exactamondo dearest Pet,' sayz I.

And so we stroll down the old Upper Lloyd.

But now, halfway down the old Upper Lloyd, my flame will not be placated no more.

I kung-fuey Petra in the back.

She falls, like a toddler, over and onto her hands, bewildered.

'Oh no! Oh no!' sayz Mid, more alarmed by the obvious tregateurie of the Blyton playground like handshaking of a moment before.

'No, leave them,' sayz Georgia. 'Leave them to

fight it out,' sayz she.

And so I pulls out the sliver of the blade that keeps my hair back and off my face and wave it around in front of her.

She does the same.

Blyton types pass in their electric moving boxes. But this is a common enuff sight on their way home, rushing to be back in the safety of their own land.

Petra knows my moves too well.

Bitch.

But I catch her fingers right across and she is more amazed now by the trickle of blood that is, like her, drip drip dripping onto the cold winter pavement.

'No more!' sayz she, dropping her blade, her hair now down round her waist – the fallen grrrl that she is – I didn't just rely on the blade to keep my hair back in its place – I have extra support – the blade isn't to be relied on alone.

Undignified.

'Right middling Middie, your turn now!' I shoutz. She nearly shitz herself, poor Middie. But she falls right into character. She screamz to convey her angria. And then takes out the blade from her hair – now, I has to give credit where credit is due – her hair stays in place. She hasn't relied on the blade as her only support. She lunges straight forward and her blade whooshes past my face. I can hear Petra stopping Georgia from bounding in to protect me with her Gypsy bare knuckle tactics. I too lunge forward, and she is, literally, taken aback, and I slash a large line in the front of her overalls.

Blood drips down her zip.

It is as if she isn't used to seeing her own blood, dear sistaz, if anyone is used to see the old scarlet, it is us, isn't it?

Anyhoo . . . she panics, and screams and scrikes like a little bambino babby.

Hee haw, hee haw.

'Oh no, no,' cries Petra. Georgia pats me on the shoulder, to say 'well done'.

'But she's bleedin' really very bad,' sayz Petra, now crouched down at Mid's side.

'It's not the first time – 'twon't be the last,' sayz I.

'But we can't leave her here, she might die!' sayz she.

'She was dead before she came into our arena,

dear grrrl.'

But I takes a black square of hankie from my top pocket and tapes it firmly in place to Mid. 'Tisn't even deep enough for the old orphery skills.

'Silly girlie wirlie,' sayz I.

We arrive at Gutshot Rebos – and I order a good old pick me up tonic for the two fighters, but no speedy weedy extra for them, only for me and Georgia. There is no reason for us to miss out on kick starting our Phrontisteries.

On our way back we stop off at The Duchess of New York on McColl. The muvvafukkaz are sat in a group in their usual corner. Tut tuts and raised eyes all around please muvvaz!

'Barman! Four aquas for your four favourite aquabibs,' sayz I.

'Water nonsense!' Gloria sayz.

'Actu-alie,' Petra sayz . . . 'I'll have a gin and . . . gin.'

'A gin and gin?' I asks.

'Double gin.'

'Double gin?'

'I'll have what she's having too,' Mid pipes up.

Georgia shakes her head.

'That's it girls, a good drink never done no one any harm,' my dearest muvva calls over.

The barman serves the two aquas and the two double gins. They can hardly be told apart, except two are in shorter glasses. Mid, as if scared it's going to disappear as fast as her courage is threatening to, grabs the glass of gin and knocks it back, almost in one.

'You drink that like a true muvvafukking expert, perhaps we should call you Madame Geneva?' sayz I.

'Look Alex, yeah, the odd drink isn't gonna turn us into our muvvafukkas,' sayz Petra. Mid nods her head in agreement, whilst staring into the glass, studying it for traces left, like a coke whore on her knees on the carpet of a party full of cold sufferers.

The drip behind the bar makes himself busy, arranging the array of stained glass bottles, dusting the glass shelves.

Gloria, it seems, isn't even interested in her daughter's wound. For her, it is nothing to having to leave Blyton and take up in Moss-Side. She seems more proud of her daughter's double gin swigging than anything else.

Hee hee haw haw.

She has truly had to buy into relativism.

Perspectivism.

The others – ours.

'Gonna buy your poor old muvvaz a drinkie winkie then?' me own muvva calls out from behind a cloud of smoke.

A plan quickly forms in my mind.

I order the drip to pour four stouts *for* the stouts.

'Come on Grrrlz,' sayz I, and march out of the old Duchess of New York.

6

We run down McColl and up Wilmslow and still, like little US Jar Heads, one-two all the way to Owens' Park, which is the biggest joke on us Moss-Side philosophers, for 'tis the exclusive residential domain of the old professori types and old Greer-like women.

Our target for the night is well in sight.

It is a large old Edwardian type house – enough to hold about ten of the Moss-Side Block 2 flatettes.

More, even.

There are triangles of light resting on tall spikes. The sign sayz:

'Mrs. Gaskell's Academy for Girls'

The main windows have burglar bars on them.

The iron has been moulded into flowers and stem like things – how these people have to delude themselves.

Decoration.

Ornament.

Protection.

We peer into a few of the windows. Posters on the wall of different countries that require Blyton passports.

Cave ab homi ne unius li bri

runs around the room in fancy old script. Well, I would be ok then! I move onto a lit window and view what is the school kitchen. I see an old Greer-like pouring the old rich calf-juice into saucers for an army of little yapping yapper bag-dogs.

Aaaahhhh.

The headmistress, I presume.

And theyz fatter than most of the people of the Moss-Side Blocks.

And they jump up and down at will – on the large granite worksurfaces, on the big old rustic butcher's block table fingie, all yap-yapping to get to the old calves-juice.

I can eye, through the kitchen and into a corridor, all the oldey worldey ornaments and cuckoo clocks that have long ceased to be crafted with loving hands. Well, we are going to get crafty enough.

'OK, we're gonna ask for some aqua first, we'll see if she gives us poor fings some water, after seeing to her little yap yappers,' sayz Georgia. She is well into this sort of stuff. It is an insult to her and her own, to see this level of decadence – she is well up for it.

I sayz to Petra and Mid, 'You two, stand either side of the big grandey door, yes?'

They nod, yes yes. I has to be careful with these two Madames Geneva.

I bang on the mascaron, hideous that it is, like half pug-dog, half wrinkled old lush, then push the glorious doorbell that is like a rat infested old piano.

The school becomes quiet, like all their ears are still under arrest from the bell.

But too long a paws.

So I rings again.

And I call in my best voice.

'Yoo-hoo, helloooo there, I'm dreadfully very very sorry and all that, but my sister here, she has fainted and fallen right on the floor – please can you let me fone for medic?' Her slippered feet, which looked like theyz been made from polar bear come closer and closer.

In a very high pitched tone she sayz, 'Go away, go away I tell you, or I'll have to notify the authorities!'

Georgie giggles then holds her hand over her mouth.

It is time, my dear sistaz, to up the tempo.

'Oh! I'm sorry for scaring you missis, but it's my friend, heeelllpp, purrlllllease, help, she's fainted and fallen on the floor.'

'Go away, I know you're not Gaskell girls . . . Capers is what you are up to, I can smell it a mile away, selling more useless stuff door to door, shouldn't be allowed,' sayz she.

'But pleeeezzzzzzzzzzze!' sayz I.

'Go away, I say, or I'll set my doggies on you!' Georgia runs to the side of the house – so much giggling she is doing. I have to hold my own breath for a little while – for fear of uncontrollable fit of giggle wiggles. Mid doesn't see anything funny at all. Probably reminds her of some old woman she used to get on well wiv in Blyton or summat.

'OK then, sorry to bother you, we'll just have to find helpful help someplace else. Come dear sister, we'll find some help somewhere, I hope I can lift you on my own,' sayz I.

I can feel the old biddie's presence by the door, waiting, listening.

'Mid! Wire!' I whisper. She does. Within five minutes we are in a side window.

Hee hee. Haw haw.

It is a good time.

It is Compulsory Recovery Hour and so the streets are empty. I drop, with all the grace of a cat, hee hee, into a side corridor, full of dust it is. These Blytons, don't know how to maintain what they have. And I pass five class-rooms – all empty – what a waste! My forts turn to the earlier horror of Mid and Petra, and I decide, right there and then, to do it all on me ownsie – placate the oldie, shut the yap yappers up if needs be, although, it has to be said, my dear sistaz, that I have nothing against them as such, and then simply take as much loot as poss. Think of the enchiridions stashed up in this place. Gerald-o will trade some in for me.

Doing it solus would show them who is the leader.

117

I is worth all three of 'em put together.

Of that I is sure.

I arrive in the doorway of this grand old room, what would once have been called a drawing room. 'The Mistress's drawing room . . . The Mistress will see you now'. The old Greer-like sits on a chaise longue, with a big old cane in her hand.

'Hello there, sorry you couldn't find it in yourself to help me and my friend,' sayz I.

'GET OUT, GET OUT, GET OUT!' she shrieks, and begins to wave the cane around. I pick up a stack of enchiridions that are at the foot of a grand piano. And then my eyes fall on a first edition of *The Driver's Seat*, by long expired Muriel Spark, which I had been taken with when first read. I make to grab at it.

She whacks me across the back.

I swipe the book and then leap through the room, much niftier than the old Greer-like.

She continues to bang bang the old stick on the old oak furniture that hasn't seen a duster for many a year.

'GET OUT, THIS SCHOOL ISN'T FOR PEOPLE LIKE YOU – YOU SHOULDN'T BE IN THIS AREA – IT'S FOR REAL PEOPLE

– FOR PROPER PEOPLE. IT. IS. FOR. GASKELL. GIRLS.' sayz she.

'AND LOTS OF DOGZ!' sayz I. I prance down the long corridor on either side of which are the old classrooms and lecture theatres, through the big old kitchen and am halted when I slide in one of the yappers accidents! The yap yappers are being a tad bad tempered, growling like little grizzlies in a growlery. Before I know it I feel as though my head is caving in. She launches the cane into me again – about my head; I drop the book. Then I hear old cop sirens in the distance.

At first I sphynx it is just my head making funny noises. Bent down, I run to the main door and pull back a whole series of pieces of metals. One. Two. Three. Four.

There, on the doorstep is Mid.

'What's going on here then Middling-Mid?' I asks. I catch sight of Georgia and Petra running into the dark distance.

Oh, I finks. Mid has waited for me.

Aaaahhh!

Then Mid pulls out her blade and slashes me across the face.

Whilst I am reeling from shock she runs off after the other two tregateurs.

I count seven seconds exactly. Why. I do not know. The big cop van and cop car pull up by the front door.

Where I am still stood.

Stood still.

'Right you, little Alex, you slag! We're having you!' sayz the old bull dykey cop woman. They pull me, my dear sistaz, hither and tither, all over the show, bang me head against the doors of the van, then against the sides of the inside of the van. Then punch me in the stummick – bang, bang, bang, bang, bang, bang, bang, bang, bang. I is their new stress ball. I kick out from the back – like the ass I now feel. I can feel their angria, their unresolved reservoirs of angria as they punch and hit and kick and bang and punch and hit and kick and bang.

'We got you now you little bitchslagslutcuntbastardbitchscum,' they all sayz.

'Get the others, theyz in The Duchess of New York slurping gin-gins. *GET THEM*!' I callz out, now livid and half breathless. And, despite the beatings, in a moment of pure haecceity I realise the extent of the tregateurie.

'Never mind trying to detract attention away from yourself you little scumbitchbastardcuntslutslag-bitch,' this one sayz.

My three so called fellow Grrrlz had all been drinkers, little alchies all along – just like their own muvvafukkas. What chance did I have? Did we have? Well, I don't care what mess I am now in. It's no different from the mess I have always been in. And it won't end here, my dear sistaz, no way! I am still on my Journey.

The van, wiv me going bang bang bang from side to floor to side to floor to side in the back, moves off, jolting all over the show, wiv them cozzas all laff, laff, laffing.

FUCKINGBITCHSCUMBASTARDTWATS CUNTSCOZZAS.

7

I needn't share wiv u lot how my muvvafukka hasn't shown up for me. I never expected the old bitch to either.

So there!

Then, in the middle of my place on the old pittypot my ears become offended by some old warbly vocals of an old bitch:

And a chorus of voices come into play and shouts back:

'SHUTTHEFUCKUPSTUPIDOLDIRISH BITCHBASTARDBITCHSHUTUPSHUT ITSHUTYOURDIRTYOLDCAKEHOLE FUCKINGSTUPIDBITCH'. And then there is far more screaming: owowowowowowow owow, heeeeeeelllpppppp!

A Milly Molly Bandy like cop hands me a hand-mirror with a smirk.

I check my face.

It is unrecognizable. Just like a mascaron. It is swollen and purple, and a slight hue of blue here and there, and a bit of black under the eyes and over the eyes, and a gush of dried blood leading from my mouth down my chinny chin chin and down my long Grecian neck, creating quite a nice contrast against the alabaster like skin of my neck.

My face no longer knows the meaning of alabaster, only pebbledash.

That's when I am 'greeted' by a tall, wide cop man, which is unusual enough, and he has big fuck off stars all over his shoulders. And he holds his hands behind his wide back and arches one eyebrow to show that the power is ON in him and OFF in me.

BASTARD!

'I WON'T SPEAK UNTIL MY SOLICITOR GETS HERE,' sayz I – even though I don't have one. Can't have one. One of the cop women side-kicks comes over and rams her disgusting fist into me stummick.

The big man laffs to see such fun, hee hee hee hee hee hee, and the cow jumps over the moon. And so, the minute she turns her smug stupid facey back to her OUR MEN boss I kung fuey her in the back and over she falls – onto him. I then grab her and bang her head against the cell wall. BANG. BANG. BANG. All my RAGE barathrumic.

HE HE WHORE WHORE!

Well, she's not rite happy with that. But she slides down and collapses into a heap.

And then they all set on me. Theyz know they can do no more to my face so they grab my arm and, in turn, ram me against one wall, and then another, and then another, stepping over the heap in the middle of the cell – and this ring a ring a roses malarkey goes on for about mmmm, eight and a half minutes.

That's when they stop.

'I think she's done her in!' one of them sayz, checking the dum dum on the floor.

'And rightly so,' sayz I.

'You're scum you are,' sayz one. And spits in my face. There is no way I am gonna behave like some little boy and try and seek their approval. No, theyz can all fuck right off. And so I fold my arms and give my best Mona Lisa smile.

It hurts though.

Blinking hurts. And as I sit here I just think I'm so glad I've been against you and everything you represent – you shower of kunts.

The body of the dum dum is removed in stunned silence. I am left in the cell – alone, they said to 'sphinx over the life sentence you will now automatically serve', but the only fings I can sphinx over are *my* injuries and my own splatters of blood on the floor and walls. There is no way I am going to conform to THEM, to THEIR way – even if it meanz my days are no more.

It's amazing what angria can do.

It gives resolve – *energy*.

Power – ON.

I am even more resolved, my dear sistaz.

Hee hee haw haw.

They are the herd.

And, we, dear sistaz, we are the unheard.

Like Star Rover I let myself play in me own Phrontistery.

The herd versus the unheard.

The herds of unheard.

Un-her'd.

Un'her'd?

Gilligan voiced a different voice – the sexes are
unlike in mind *and* body. Un. Like. In body.

Yes.

And. Mind.

Minded?

Two ways of . . . x 2 voices.

Females fear separation.

Fee males.

Theme. Ales. Fear.

The theme of ales is fear.

Here. *Hear.*

Cultural femme. Cult of femme.

Same arguments. Different languages.

RE branding.

Always. Re: bra ending.

Men reason. Women feeling.

Oppression rationalization. Self. Full. Filling.
Professoris. Social beliefs.

If only social be leaf!

Bereft. Left. Alone. Alone. Alone. Known. All *is
known.* Alone. Own. Acorn. Grow. Tree. Free. Me.
Goddess. Not less. *More.* The Dark Continent.
Freud. Fraud.

Yawn.

BORED.

Balls! They're all Kunts.

Feeling. Reason. *Feeling* reason enough to emote. Move. Shift. *Change!*

I am just enjoying me own diss of course when a few of them return with a fully typed up statement that I am s'posed to have spoken.

But haven't.

They point a pen at me and sayz 'SIGN.'

They make me.

What can I do? Yes, yes, I know *'tis* me. But not YET! Not in legal fact, eh?!

Then they take me out of solitary cell and put me in big communal cell with ten other women, pushing me and punching me as I go along.

I sneer at them – most of them are old muvvas. One of them is sayin' to this uvver one, 'Yeah but, like, it isn't me fault, lah – I'd relapsed – on sugar, yeah, is buzzin' and all that, 'tis the sugar I tell you,' she sayz. 'Yeah, yeah,' sayz the other, nodding at her, but not listenin', only workin' out how she could present *her* case when there is eventually a gap of silence between the two. Practicing their own rhetoric for the court room under the guise of dialogue. A group of three are huddled in the corner. And she said she'd been stressed out on a spending binge – a *what* binge? I fort.

And then anuvva cries out for drink, then two minutes later gets on her knees and keeps saying, 'I admit I am powerless dear God our Farva, over King Alcohol and that my life has become, like, too fucking damn unmanageable.' Me, I huddles up in a corner and rests my sore head against the dirty-like-you've-never-seen-dirty-before wall, and closes me sore eyes. And sleep.

I am being shoved, by a cop's foot, 'WAKE UP THERE YOU!' sayz she.

'But Miss tell them, missie, I have admitted it is the alcohol - it's a disease, not my fault,' the earlier woman is spouting, pulling at the sleeve of the cop.

'FUCK OFF!' the cop tells *her* and then kicks *me* again. **'WAKE UP – the headmistress of Mrs. Gaskell's Academy for Girls is pressing charges of trespass, but our colleague is DEAD! Murdered by YOU! And you're in BIG TROUBLE! GET UP AND GET OUT!'** she shouts. The cell has gone quiet. What I have done dwarfs all their deeds combined. This woman, and a big square shouldered man, push me to a solitary cell at the back of the station, where the walls are, apparently, reinforced against bombs and the like. Do I care that I have murdered a dum dum doing her job? Yes. I would. But she wasn't doing her job. D'ya get me?

PART TWO

1

If you want to know what real injustice is – this is where it begins, my dear sistaz. I have been given, rent free, a little cell in the Moss-Side Women's Prison, which is actually somewhere in the middle of nowhere and nowhere near the area that reared me. Theyz just named it that because it has been built just for us.

And I say they never do anysphinx for us.
Aaaaahhhhhh!

I don't sphinx I need to point out that I have received no visitors yet – not even me own muvva has taken the time to leave the miasma at the Old Duchess of New York to visit her one and only.

I am luckier than all the rest of the sad cases in here – I have my learned understanding and my memorized lines of inspiration and fighting fuel, and poetry – which is far more valuable than the smeggy family members that are visiting the other saddos. I'd rather recite Langston Hughes 'what happens to a dream deferred', over and over and over than sit facing my muvva's ugly mug only to hear her whingeing on and on about how having me not only tore her body in two, but also ruined her life – as though the situation she had been born into would ever have meant anysphinx different – stupid old kunt.

And I have even started having these, like, really weird, disturbing dreams about Heathcliffe and Cathy and Wuthering Heights.

And in these dreams, which are rather recurrent, I do the old Kate Bush voice and scream on top of the wind swept moors – my hair down to my waist, 'Heathcliffe, it's me, it's Cathy, I've come home, I'm so coooooooooolllld, let me into your windowwwww,' and all that razzamatazz.

But enough of the Freudian slippages here there and everywhere.

In this prison I have been banged up with a load of muvvafukking child beaters and neglectors and all that barkey marlarkey – and some of them are pulling their hair out for alchiehol, drugs, sugar, caffeine, and even bibles.

But no escapism here girlie wirlies.

But I do, escape that is, all in me head. They'd have to take me brain out of its case to get me where they wanted! And so I get these funny looks as I walk along the landings; possessor of secret and illicit poetry and literature and wisdom and purpose rocket fuel. My flame, my dear sistaz, has not died, but has remained loyal, like a yare lighthouse in days of yore, constantly flash flash flashing out to sailors in need. Except there are no sailors. Obviously.

Then there is the trial.

And I is given twenty-one years *minimum*.

Twenty-one. And that's if I'm, like, *good!*

For me that must be almost another lifetime. I argue with the judge in the court, this old bastard man with beady old eyes. I ask him would he have given that sentence to a seventy year old, and he massaged his chinny chiny chin and sayz, mmmmm, yes, I think so. And then I sayz, but that's not even a third of his entire life to date and he wouldn't live long enough to serve it, and yet it's almost an entire lifetime to date for me. Then he sayz, yes but he could die in there, or even if she/he got out at eighty-four what could he do?

I have to concede that it was a slightly fair point.

I thank him for the little debate, and off I go to begin my prison paragraph, page, book – for sentence it is not. And so I is no longer referred to as Alex, but 210773.

What can be done?

I have been in this lock up for nigh on two years. Twenty three months to be exactamondo.

We are hit at will by the warders and older prisoners. And lots of bull-dykes are just dying to get their big yellow stained gnarled hands on a Grrrl like moi. Then we spend most of each and every day, six days a week, assembling nuclear gadgetry that is updated every six months 'to keep the economy going' and which the Blytons are obliged to buy 'to keep the economy going' and which are put together by us for nothing 'to keep the economy going'. It is a system of gombeens created by a gregatim of gombeens.

In the evenings they have us doing pottery and embroidery – always hand work sayz they, good for defective minds, is hand work. And the way they sayz it, it's like it should be some sort of feile or somesphinx.

I once asked them what they fort of my handiwork on the old dum dum.

But I had me head banged against the wall.

Poetry and philo niceties rattled, but still safe tho'.

Hee hee haw haw. Then, after all this time, the prison warder comes in to notify me of my muvvafukkaz visit. I tell the prison warder bitchface that I is to receive no visitors today – no time to stop the flow that keeps 'the economy going', sayz I. I have my head banged against the wall and am told, if I don't want to see her, then I damn well must, coz that'd be what it is like in hell and that's where I waz goin' so I'd better damn well get used to it. Another witticism leapt about on the tip of my tongue. But, I thinks, I'll save it, keep it in the bank. Me muvva sits there, looking even more haggard and wino like. Smoking her head off like a choo choo chug chug.

'Georgia's dead,' she sayz. 'That caravan site they insisted on living in had been set on fire, that's how they went, the lot of them, up in flames, the dogs ran off and then were shot for being out on their own without a lead. I don't know, you shoulda seen it.'

Well, my sistaz, I can't say I'm not affected. Like I sayz before, Georgia has been like a sista to me and, even though she had turned tregateur, she is the one I fort was closest to me.

Oh, my dear sistaz, the fickle hand of fate and fortune. Georgia is now off the face of this hell-hole earth. And I has to admit, I am glad for her, d'ya get me, lah? She would.

*

I am in the prison chapel. The priestess of God the Farva is sharing with us the Word to be Heard from the Lord hisssself.

Me, as I am one of the only one out of us all in'mates' that can read, has been given the task of Reader. It is okay, I can hone my skills of oratory and rhetoric – emphasizing the insanity of the book of Job at various/ numerous points so that the prisoners would, yeah, be almost wetting themselves with disbelief at this night-mare of a jackanory. There is only one reading per Sunday service. Not nearly enough, if you ask me, but it means that I get extra time to myself to read the Word, that is, the Bible of our Wholly Farva and choose ten minute Reader pieces each week. Even if that does mean having to listen to the sermonizing of this Priestess of the Holy Farva.

'Are you young women (Young Women, *d'ya get me?* Condescension at its finest) gonna spend your lives in and out of institutions and the like? Have you no respect for yourselves?' she asks. 'Don't you know that there is far more punishment in the next world than in this?'

Well, that's me done for then, if the next world is as bad, nay, **worse** than this, then I'm damned to damnation,' I sayz to meself; but I am an Aesthete instead – no, not an atheist, or an agnostic, just an aesthete of the word.

Of the knowledge.

'Did you know hell exists?' the priestess asks, like she is Elizabeth Gaskell trying to save the souls of nineteenth century factory ants and raggety whores. Not realizing she is nought but a haggedy bore.

'Yes, we've spent our whole lives innit, innit!' pipes up one voice.

I giggles.

As does everyone.

And, my dear sistaz, these are not the grizzly cynical giggles of the knowing, but the vulnerable, unexpected giggles of little girlies.

It has hit home.

'Well . . . well . . . that's nuffin' compared to what

you've put uvvers through on this earth,' sayz the priestess. Continuing in her most Blytonesie voice of solemnity, she begins to spout more words, of redemption, sinning, rabbiting on about the importance of the Protestant work ethic which is at the heart of keeping 'the economy going', just as Ballard had prophesied in his Subliminal Man – of which we have never been a part of anyway; and Heaven and Hell, the latter we are going to see, the former we most definitely are not.

Anyhoo . . . after the service the priestess comes up to me and I let her sermonize me, her little pitiful one – the possible Mary of Magdalene whom Jesus had managed to love despite her being a total slutbag, unlike her more questionable sista/cousin, or whoever the Hell she is, the one who said that the baby had just got there without any nastiness thank you very much.

'Thank you for the reading today, it was most appropriate for you young women of Moss-Side, thank-you again 210773,' sayz she, and squeezes my arm and looks deep into my eyes in a smarmy Blytonesie pseudo-sincere but patronising kinda way. I can smell veeno on her breath. I had wondered why she had so many broken veins across her facey.

Shoulda known. If I'm an expert on anything now, it's that. Surely.

Anyhoo . . . she gave me the bible and sayz, 'Choose just as aptly for next week . . . and you are on your way to a genuine desire to become a good person of our state,' she adds.

I just thinks, 'yeah, and what a state!'

'If you continue like this, being on the RIGHT side, you'll get early release for goodie goodie behaviour. Twenty-one years, if you're lucky.'

I do my most humblest look of humiliation, just like I imagine Mary Magdalene had to be before the men who had paid her now said she is ok enuff to be accepted back into their world. And off she goes, no doubt to peek a little nippie of the old drinkie winkie woo woo.

I make my way back to my cell in order to choose 'as aptly' for the next service. V.V., the vinegar-faced guard, allows me to trundle off away on me own whilst she catches up on some gossip with the Priestess of God the Farva. Drinkers both! I linger awhile, behind the mock-sacristy and listen to what they mutter, one never knows when gossip serves as the most valuable currency.

'You have the patience of a saint, sister,' the guard tells the Priestess.

'Goodness has to be strove for, Vera, worked for and prayed for, which they seem not to have caught the hang of just yet. If they ever will. Dear dear. But we mustn't judge!'

This holiest of holies pours two glasses of wine and they each take a long sip – a glug-glug. 'Aaahhhh,' they both go.

'But it's easy saying that, not so easy in practice, and now they talk about this new rehabilitation programme in the silver building.'

'Aaah, so they are going ahead with it then, how sad,' the Priestess says, and pours them both more of the old communion veno.

'You know all about it then?' V.V. asks.

'Have done for quite some time, it's been an ongoing debate, and now they seem to have pushed it through, well, it's called the Bill 'N' Bob technique,' sayz she, saying it in a wary, lower voice, as though it is the devil itself.

V.V. shakes her head and purses her lips, loosening them only to take another glug-glug.

'It's been very big over the pond,' Priestess sayz, then whispers, 'Some say it's the new religion, Bill 'n' Bobbites.' I see her fall into a strange land far away from Moss-Side Women's Prison, as if sphinxing over that strange and impending new religion, just like Mid used to.

'Ooh,' sayz V.V.

'Yes, ooh indeed,' sayz she, coming back to the world of Moss-Side Women's. 'But, it's only in the experimental stage as far as the prisoners are concerned, you see, but they hold great promise by it, apparently, not for me though . . .' sayz she.

'It's an OUT-rage. It shouldn't be allowed. What are they playing at? They'll put us out of a job, that's for starters . . .' V.V. sayz.

'When a girl, or woman, cannot choose to be good, Vera, then she must have been invaded by satan itself,' sayz she.

'And they need to be kept away from normal decent society for as long as possible, by US!' V.V. sayz.

I have a stream of monologue racing thru my Phrontistery right now, dear sistaz, a ten point crissy-crossy put down. A group of dejected, hunched over inmates file in now for their bit of the Our Men grand narrative. Now, wot I is sphinxing here is that a girl, or woman, who cannot see beyond the Our Men bollox and who has no fire in her belly about this, well, she has no right to even have a Phrontistery.

D'ya get me, lah?

'Ooh now, more gregatim to tend,' sayz Priestess, and slugs back the rest of the veno and wipes out her silver chalice thing with a crisp white starched cloth.

Gregatim is right, thinks I.

Offs I toddles, back to my cell to think well, on all I have heard and to choose my next reading. Vinegar Vera catches up quick.

'What are you doing there, come on, get a move on, no dilly-dallying,' sayz she.

I turn and face said screw and, with my most saintliest of smiles, but not the mad deluded upside lip arc of mad old Joan, I hold up God's enchridion and sayz, 'Jackanory from the Good Book, a task and a half, in these dayz, is it not?'

'SHUT IT!' she shouts back and slams metal door behind her. But that, dear sistaz, is not what power is all about, not about the slammin' of a metal door, no, no, no. It's all in the old Phrontistery, d'ya get me? And all played out on the level of the old mentalese, a level on which, if winning, is a room of solid gold and all the heart could ever desire. However, for me, and those who saw beyond the mere appearance of such things, that superior level in the palace of mentalese is cool, clear, pre-Reyjakiv tourist Iceland personified. Like a long glass of cool, clear, clean water amidst a sea of fizzy, neon toxicity.

I sits meself down, and then opens the Good Book.

It is a book.

Ergo, it is Good. Interpretation is another matter entirely.

It opens at The Proverbs – pro verb, pro action, proactive. I play, proactively. With the words. It is, my dear sistaz, if there is one god damn fing to be learnt from those old grey men whose language we are left with, it is play – with words, as long as it suits them – like woe of man – s and r, appendages of he. To know wisdom, and instruction; to perceive the words of understanding. To instruct, know and wisdom, to stand under the words – to perceive – structures, fuck their strictures.

Strictures only of structures.

That is the Word – *d'ya get me?*

My daughter, hear NOT the instruction of thy mother, and forsake not her law.

For it is poor.

And more.

Stricture only structures.

For she is of them.

For that they loved knowledge, and did NOT choose the fear of the Lord!

Halle-fucking-looyah!

She *is* more precious than rubies: and all the things thou canst desire are not to be compared unto her.

Indeed.

Full stop.

Word Up!

What reading?

It shall, my dear sistaz, have to be played safe, St. John or St. Matthew – something about wolves in sheep's clothing – or, sheep that become wolves depending on their state/corporate uniform. The Phrontistery always has ways and meanz of interpretation through the filter of freedom! But the Filter of Freedom can, my dear sistaz, only do so much, as within cannot extend to without in such circumstances as I now find myself in – as each of my fellow Moss-Side Women prisoners enters what is also their cell. If we were not known only by filthy number I would call meself Moll, not as in Gangsta's, but Flanders. Conditions not altogether different. No hay or shit on floor. Nor a saucy, ironic, debt-ridden narrator. But cattle treatment nonetheless.

Even the cattle prod.

Even the churchey type, pushing for repentance – salvation – the possibility – the pushing of the potential of a 'new' life that is more aligned to THEIRS.

And then, my dear sistaz, I could, even then, feel my fate about to take another turn. This evening, just a short while ago, one of the warders stood before my cell door, a big fat grin across her face. I still had the enchiridion in my hand. She signalled for me to leave the cell and stand in a corner. With her.

'You, 210773, will no longer read the Readings, unless . . . unless you are willing to grant me . . . favours. Comprende?'

I knew it! Well, Etna reared up like a woman scorned, and hell hath no fury and all that, and so I launched into this messenger where no word can suffice and let her have it. I pushed her against the wall. Then I allowed myself to let go and hails my punches into the squish of her skin and the bang of her bone. It was, I imagined, like working dough in an old bakery – I just couldn't stop; it felt like a mist had descended and didn't exactly fire me up, but, as Etna had kept me fired up, this launching of fists was cooling me down – the one needing the other. Hot passion/Cold reason. Until I was grabbed and pulled off. Which would, I had known, only mean more of the same. And I. DO. NOT. CARE. But even now, several hours later, I know it is too late. Not for me. But for her.

2

There reigned a stunned silence in the thirty minutes after. I have killed her. The guard who had the unfortunate idea, and yes, she had taken gleeful gladness from that idea, of telling me that I would no longer be allowed to choose and read the Readings, unless I granted her 'special' favours.

'You shouldn't . . .' I had begun.

'SHUT IT!' I am ordered. Commanded. Told.

I nods my noggin' and shakes me face.

Despair.

And where?

And what?

And she is/was a dyke. I could smell it a mile off. Overbearing daddykins and weak mummykins – opposite of the gay man's overbearing muvva and weak farva!

Fervour!

Man murder.

I had known it from day one. Really. In she came, on my first day, with a blue dot, on each of her pitifully once fragile female knuckles – Indian ink rebellion half covered in the state blue guard's uniform – I have no time for it, my dear sistaz, this, this, half-way branding . . . handing it over to THEM!

LOVE/HATE
MUM/DAD
MAN/WOMAN
HATE/STATE
BLYTON/MOSS-SIDE
SNIDE.

'And you!' she had said, this illiterate, minimum wage hag, pointing one of her branded fingers AT me!

AT ME!

I sat atop my mount Etna, telling her to be still, there would be a time for her expression of fire. Wouldn't there just.

She pointed again – AT me!

'You, sleep in the corner – on the floor,' she had said. And this, yeah, was all on day ONE, what a welcome!

The uvvers in the cell had laffed – like workmen looking at plastic tits in a caff.

'Not unless you wanna be my bitch!' she had added.

Well, she had given up that first time, but there had been other times, little touches here and there. And all the while I had bided my time. And then, using the Readings of the Voice and the Word. Well. That had to be the final straw. *Need I say more?*

Well?

I is put into me own cell. Solus. Perfect.

There's always a bright side, in't there? And the entire prison is under lock down. Or lock up.

Whatevver.

I, dear sistaz, after being tainted by the red brush of murderous blame, was then taunted by a procession of screws through the hole in the door, and even kicked a few times inside my so called solus cell.

I did point out that I is s'posed to be in solus confinement.

Solus.

Confinement.

But I is told I is to SHUT IT!

That I had an ANSWER FOR EVERYTHING.

I sayz if they fort that I have an answer for everything, then why did theyz not listen to my answers, then?

You see what sense these people make? None!

Hee hee whore whore.

Now. Coming towards the end of my first full day of no beatings, I finally gets some sleepie bye byes. ZZZZZZZZZZZZZZZZZZZZZZZZ.

The next morning I am awoken early. I hears the feet of men. Official men. Heavier, denser plates of meat. And then, a slight trail of giggle wiggles from the troop of accompanying screws. He whore, He whore!

I stays where I am.

Well, don't have much choice now, do I?

But I is soon gonna, my dear sistaz, I is soon gonna, I can feel the anticipation of change in the air like a subtle change in the weather that I no longer get to feel/see. Some of my fellow inmates, I can hear, are doin' the old dirty calls through from behind their doors - sayin' they can smell the meatheads and all that jazz.

I don't know about meatheads but I know that

I can smell extra perfume from the screws, trailin' behind them like. Per'aps you'd have fort I'd have kept me mouth shut, what wiv bein' in solus conf and all that. But no.

AS IF!

I clears me throat, daintily, cannot stand bad manners in me own company, and then, at the top of me voice, I shouts,

'Keep the fuckin' noise DOWN!' And I meanz it too. It is comedic.

For two seconds the audio landscape changes – from din din din, to silence is golden, golden . . .

Even the footsteps have stopped.

But, like I say, 'tis only for two secondos and, on the third the footsteps are like, trying to bore their way through the iron or steel whatever the hell it is, floor, in their attempt to choo choo their way to my cell door. Hee hee. Haw haw.

BANG BANG! on the door, which, incidentally, is made of same hardy type material as the floor.

I stand right in front of the square grid as it is opened by a Vinegar Vera screw, but not too right in front of it, if you get me drift, wouldn't want to damage my face with an accidental swipe of her truncheon, and there is plenty more of that now that I have done in one of their own. Her face lurches in at me, her eyes wrinklier and wrinklier as they squint in at me before she is abruptly pushed out of the way and a middle-aged Blyton man looks in - his eyes an electric blue, as if to say, 'Who the fuck are you?' But I am thinking the same of him.

'Drugs?' he asks.

'Just say NO!' repliez little old me.

'NOT YOU!' he sayz. He, apple-arently, isn't talkin' to me, but to his colleague, the guvnor-ette.

'Of course,' sayz she, in a higher than usual pitch. Mascaron bitch. Tregateur.

'Alchie-hol too?' he adds, still gawping in at me.

I shakes me head. Dum dums I thinks.

'Absolutely!' the guvnor-ette replies.

I'm now thinkin', her voice can't reach any higher. I let them sphinx what they likes most of the time - why it's energy that could be spent on the old Phrontistery, bish bash boshing? Theyz just assumes we have taken up the sins of our muvvas.

Fukkaz!

'Well, she could be just perfect for Dr. Groome's highly regarded, well established Bill 'n' Bob Technique,' he sayz, turning now, away from me, to Mrs. Bitch High-Pitch. 'If it could work on such a case as this it could work on *anyone*.'

I hears this tho' and know just exactamondo what it meanz.

'I'm goin' nowhere,' sayz I, using a bit of the old reverso psycho.

OH.

YES.

YOU.

ARE!

Mrs Guvnor-ette Bitch now Low-Pitch sez.

'Good! Splendid. We have our first! Many more will follow from here,' sayz the man, and he and Mrs Guvnor-ette trundle along the landing back to her office where she will no doubt jump him like he's never been jumped before.

'You'll be out of here this afternoon then, you scheming little bitch, the Bill 'n' Bob technique me arse! Next they'll be wrappin' yuz all up in cotton wool and sayin' it's not really your fault youse is bad, it's an OUTRAGE!' sayz Vinegar Vera.

'FUCK! OFF!' shouts I and lets meself slide

down the wall and onto the floor to meditate - that is, to let the old Phrontistery go mad - like London's Star Rover – once deemed a Modern Classic, but even Blyton-esque Shit-lit Chick-lit is now considered on the level with Paradise Lost!

Hee Haw! Hee Haw!

Like the good old Piccashitty Palare Mozza once said, 'Hang the DJ . . . for the music that they constantly play, it sayz nothing to me about my life, hang the blessed DJ . . .'

3

This evening, old Vinegar Vera comes and disturbs my solitude, serene that it is.

'YOU, GET UP!' shoutz she.

'Err, yeah?' asks I, not bovverin' to look upwards at her ugly mush.

'I SAYZ, GET UP NOW!' she repeats. I yawn and then slowly rise, as if from slumber, and stretch out my slender yet powerful arms, until she grabs the right one – mid air.

'OI, WATCHAFINK YOU'RE DOIN' sayz I.

'Ooh, do you know, you are common you lot in 'ere,' she sayz. Well, she'd know all about that, wouldn't she, this woman who wouldn't know Dickens from Dostoyevsky, Austen from Auster, Mitchell from Murakami – could go on but I'm sure you already catch me drift.

'It's time for you to be leavin' us once and for

all, though I don't know why they're botherin', lock 'em up and throw away the key, I sayz,' sayz she, pushing me towards the door.

'Oh good, out of here, yippee . . .' sayz I. But I turn to old Vinegar face, not yet having had my fill of pissing her off, and I asks her, 'Miss, do you sphinx we should be given a chance to rehab-il-itate, or not?'

Her eyes twitch at my impertinence.

'NO! YOU SHOULD BE LOCKED UP AND . . . AND . . .' She can see where I is going with this one, my Socratic irony coming out to play.

Hee haw. Hee haw.

'You see, it's only ever about revenge, innit,' sayz I.

'Society needs its justice,' sayz she.

'Justice is revenge though in these cases, innit, haven't I done more harm since I been in here? You don't want me to be rehabilitated because you think that's too easy, cushy, but then you don't want me to be a societal nuisance either, so, what's it to be?'

'SHUT IT AND GET GOING – too damn clever by half,' she shouts in my lug hole. I gets going then, under the additional, careful watch of another, quieter, newer screw. I laffs me head off. Some of the other girls, wimmin, whatevver, begin to call out from their own cells then:

'WHERE YA GOIN' JAMMY BITCH,' and 'TRUST YOU!' and 'IT HAD TO BE YOU, DIDN'T IT, EH!' and the like.

I am pushed along the long, steely corridor, by the long steely arm of Vinegar Vera, who pokes her long bony finger into my shoulder blade:

Dig, dig, dig.

Hag, hag, hag.

I wonder why hagiography is so saintly?!

I am made to sit and wait outside the guvnor-ette's office-ette. I am here, there, and everywhere in my good old Phrontistery. Vinegar Vera nudges me. 'OI! Stop day-dreaming! What do you think this, eh? Holiday camp?' she sayz.

'A what camp?' I asks. Sometimes they make literally no sense whatsoever.

There are traffic lights outside, on the wall. It is on red. Then amber. Then green.

'IN,' shouts V.V.

I pushes open the door only to be greeted with yet another grimster. I stand in front of her desk-ette, this bitch/bastard-ette – for she is everything

—ette/-ess. An appendage to the masculine iron fist of the state. To her, state-ette.

'Well, I suppose you know why you're here, mmmm?' she asks.

'Yes miss, no miss, three bags full miss,' sayz I with a smirk-ette.

'Oh ha ha very fucking funny, well enjoy it, yes, do, because over there isn't as cushy as you sphinx young lady,' sayz she, her breath now becoming shorter with rage.

'I never once said it was miss,' replies I.

'Well, you could be out in a fraction of the time, 28 days, apparently, *twenty-eight days*, I think they're going to find you just as impossible as we have over here, yes I do. And, once you've done away with another one of our lot, or their lot, just another decent worker, you'll be back here, or somewhere worse. Oh. Yes! There's far far worse than here, let me tell you that. In no time at all. And I have to say, off the record, that I don't agree with this Bill 'N' Bob technique whatsoever. No! There! I've said it, all you Moss-Side hardos will be sent to talk about your feelings and what then?' she asks, almost pulling her hair out with frustration.

'More civilized miss?' asks I.

'SHUT UP!' shouts V.V.

Feelings, thinks I, how glorious this trip will be, and all for twenty-eight days.

I can borrow strands from the Romantics, imagine I'm a tree having been blown around by the force of nature, creating thunderous rages and storms, stifled by the heatwaves in a barren land etcetera etcetera. An urban savage with inherent nobility. Then I could add a liberal dose of modernism, The Good Soldier that I am, though not the unreliable narrator many will think, then I could pretend to do a bit of Woolf's Septimus, sat sitting in the park musing over past battles and future internal ones, then go a bit loopy a la postmodern, let the old dream factory explore the various ontological landscapes without seeming to collapse too far into epistemological ground, if at all possible.

Mmm, yes, a treat. Star Rover, eat your fucking heart out.

'Well, that's where you are to be sent / this is all down to the government. And the state official that was here this morning,' she sayz, showing no sign whatsoever of the girly gushing of this morn. She pushes a console that is all ready on her desk towards me.

'SIGN IT,' shouts V.V. The guvnor-ette places a digi-pen, not her own silver one of course, but a crusty old plastic chewed one, next to it, and nods down for me to sign.

I picks up the console and digi-pen and begins to read it.

'WHAT ARE YOU DOING?' asks V.V.

'Reading the wordage miss,' sayz I.

'READING IT?' she asks.

'Yes, that's generally what words are for, for reading, and I need to know what I'm putting my name to.'

Well, I needn't tell you that old Vinegar V. looks like a boiler ready to explode. I turn away from and, as I is doing before so rudely interrupted, begin to read. It sayz:

'I, 210773 (Alexandra Fawley), consent to sign myself from the authority of Moss-Side Women's Prison to the State Rehabilitation Project, under the specific programme of the Bill 'n' Bob Technique for a period of twenty-eight days. However, should this period not be sufficient conversion period for satisfactory rehabilitation purposes, a second twenty-eight day period may be granted after which, if unsuccessful, transfer of mentioned prisoner back to Moss-Side Women's Prison will be made. It is, however, in the interests of the State for this plan to succeed and all endeavours will be made on the part of the State to rehabilitate said prisoner within first 28 day period, after which the prisoner will be released to enjoy her new liberty as a safe and recovered citizen . . . and must agree the terms of this programme . . . which include being available for press promotional purposes . . .

Blah Blah Blah, I am almost yawning by this point, I just know I need to show I is 'recovered' by the standards of this flowerpot men technique by the end of twenty-eight days.

I sign my name in the most elaborate, flowery script that would have been the pride of any noted Renaissance calligrapher. I look up and check out the gawping mascarons. V.V. and guvnor-ette are well and truly astounded. Fucking Neanderthals.

V.V. pushes me out of the guvnor-ette's office and makes me stand for about half an hour. And so, my dear sistaz, I meditate, but this time find a clear, blank space that can serve as a ledge upon which I can rest and restore for what is ahead. It only feels like five minutes until yet another person comes to get me. This person wears a flowery skirt and a big simple minded grin that shouts:

M A D N E S S.

Whilst mine shouts:

G L A D N E S S.

Gladness to be leaving all those vulgarities in Moss-Side nick well and truly behind me.

Me, I am about to talk about feelings, and flowers, and little hurts and recovery and all that jazz, and, in twenty-eight days, I will be free.

Four whole weeks away.

'Aah, so you're 210773, then?' she asks.

I nods.

'Well, from now on we'll give you your own name back, eh, what say you, would that be good?' she asks, as if asking an ickle Blyton kiddie winkie whether they'd prefer choccie or raspberry ice-cream.

I nods again.

'Well then Alexandra, I'm Fleur,' sez she.

'Whoa there, it's Alex, yeah?' sayz I.

'Ok then, Alex it is,' she sayz. And then I walks alongside her, down the long steely stainy corridor and out several locked doors and into the relative sunshine. We walk in silence the few minutes it takes us to get out of the prison grounds and onto the grounds of the newly built neighboring building – all silver it is. Well, I am tempted, I have to say, to jump the fence there and then, for it isn't such a strenuous sprint to the open road and all that – but, well, it is only twenty-eight days, isn't it.

We enter the clinical white building, whose walls I would love to see be adorned with a touch of the old great himself, that is, Banksy. Behind the very small, less officialesque desk in the foyer is a man with graying hair and, get this, cords, baggy cords, with a checked shirt on. Very geography teacher he is. Like Blyton gone soft, if that sorta makes sense.

I know, mad innit.

'Hello there, I'm Clive,' sayz he, and holds out his hand.

I shake it.

Reluctantly.

But, if this is all part of the twenty eight days, then . . . Then, out of a small cosy office behind him comes another man – I thought me eyes are doin' tricks on me, just that we never really saw 'em in Moss-Side.

'Hi! I'm Dr. Groome,' sayz he. Now, he is more official looking, proper trousers and all that, and older. He stares right into my face, and so I turn his male gaze right back at him with extra daggers attached, with bells on. And whistles. I can feel Mount Etna starting up before I've even got to first base. I recognize him, you see, this Dr. Groome. I have seen him on the old Recovery Channels. The ones I have watched. He is, like, some muvvafukkin' expert on the whole subject, or something.

'Now Alexandra, sorry, *Alex*, if you could sign our book here, there you go, there's a wand,' Fleur sayz and places it in my hand, directing it towards the wide screen of the incomers' register.

'Just make a cross, there,' she sayz, hovering beside me. And again, despite having a wand in my hand, I use it as one would a sixteenth century quill and elaborate even more on the loop of the 'l' and flow down heavily on one of the legs of the 'x'.

$$\boxed{Alex}$$

'Oh! I say.' Fleur sayz.

Dr. Groome and Clive come and stand beside her, keen to witness this handiwork of a now ex-inmate of Moss-Side Women's Prison.

I like to dispel stereotypes – nothing gives me greater pleasure.

Well, one greater pleasure would have to be letting loose my Phrontistery whilst creating a lovely Star of the East on a wide shopfront with a pair of Fuck Me Heels.

Hee hee. Haw haw.

'How long have you been able to write for then?' Dr. Groome interrogates. You see, there's one thing I've always been aware of when it comes to such men – theyz don't like you being a Jack-ette in the Box, or rather, theyz don't like you being a Jack-ette OUT of the box.

'Always!' sayz I, a glint in me eye.

'Nonsense! What, since the day you were born – you were born in Moss-Side, weren't you?' Clive asks, making sure the different parts of the narrative are all in place, for it is all a bit too spatchcock for his poor undernourished mind.

'YEP!' sayz I.

'Take her through then,' sayz he to Fleur, who is by now beginning to wilt, but she has to be awarded the gold medal for trying, for, despite her shoulders now hunched she compensates in tone of voice, like a neutral version of Bitch High-Pitch, 'Come on then Alex dear, I'll show you to your room,' sayz she in a sing-a-song ding dong.

'Okey dokey then,' singz I and follows her, not reluctantly like before, but now, like an eager lapdog, already tuned into the dynamics of this place.

He Whore He Whore!

I continues to follow her down long, clean white corridors that have just a splash of sickly pinkly pastel here there and everywhere – a cheap pink print on one wall, a pink cushion on a beige chair in a corner and all the doors along the corridor – white.

'Here we are then, in here,' sayz she, her voice a barometer of her interior, now wibbly wobbly WHOO WHOO!

My voice, on the other hand, is strong, even, clear.

'Okelie dokelie,' sayz I with a hey ho and a hey nonino! She leads the way into a large rectangular room, beige furniture – pink cushions. VOMIT!

'Ok then dear, Alex, sit down, do, and we'll just go through a wee bit of officialdom here,' sayz she, already switching on the screen in front of her and picking up her writing wand. 'Now, we have had all your files transferred from the prison, so we have all of that, now,' she sayz, turning to look at me, as if remembering who I am, 'but now, aah, that's what I need to do, yes, for the next seven days you'll have no contact with the others, only Dr. Groome and Ula, it's just one-on-one,' she laughs a choir mistress laugh.

Oh. Ha ha. How selcouth.

I'm fucking perplexed.

'Oh yes, you may wonder why I laugh, it's just that one-on-one, or one-to-one refers to our Step One, the most important step of our Bill 'n' Bob Technique, that's why you'll have a whole seven days just on step one, one-to-one, oh my, we never tire of the little puns on our steps here,' sayz she.

I am already tired of them.

I am beginin' to sphinx, dear sistaz, that I shoulda investigated a bit more into these 'steps', but then, how could that have been possible – talk about consumer choice, hee hee BORE BORE.

'Anyway dear, firstly we need to take some tests,

to make sure you've not taken any 'substances' in the past forty-eight hours, we know what those prisons can be like don't we, eh,' she sayz, raising her eyebrows.

'Eh?' sayz I.

'It's ok, you can tell me now if you want, oh I know you may not have had a real rock bottom lately, but, well, you're the one who's been in prison, aren't you?'

'Whoa there lady, you sayin' I'm some sort of sorry junkie?' I asks.

'NO! NO, not at all, not a sorry junkie, no, power-less addict perhaps, unmanageable alcoholic even, but sorry junkie, well, we tend not to use those terms here, it's not your fault you see, it's a *condition over which we have no control . . .*'

'WE?' I screeches. This is all going a bit too cancrizans for words.

'Yes, we, we all of us, staff included, yes, even Dr. Groome, *can you believe it?* He's wonderful really, well yes, all recovering addicts, alcoholics . . .' she sayz.

'And that's why I'm here?' I asks.

'Well, yes . . . oh I know you've only just arrived but don't worry, think nice thoughts, flowers, pinks, peaches, the denial is such a brick wall – don't worry, I identify with you, yes, that wall of denial is a tough nut to crack, but don't you worry, we're here to help YOU!' sayz she.

Well, my dear sistaz, I feel my heart slip down a chute into the basement of my stummick. So sick do I now feel to be labeled thus, there, with THEM! I think theyz rather made a mistake, theyz taken the sin of the mother and placed it on the head of the daughter. I am thinking here and now, in the wisdom of my haecceity to hold up both me hands and say, take me back to the prison, at least I can admit to what I'd done to get in THERE! But twenty-eight days, like a neon light, kept flashing in my dream factory, '**28-DAYS**' '**28-DAYS**'.

Well. I would stick it on them, I would. And then I notice, hanging on the beige wall, beside the beige blinds, an olde scrolle – it sez, in red writing, 'THE TWELVE STEPS'.

My heart, already in the basement of my being, now sinks into the pits of hell, prodded by the devil's own hot fork. I read step one, it is thus:

WE ACKNOWLEDGED THAT WE HAD BECOME CORRUPTED BY ALCOHOL/

DRUGS/WHATEVER, THAT WE, AND THUS OUR LIVES, WERE UNMANAGEABLE BY OURSELVES.

Well, dear sistaz, my rhetoric machine swung into full action. *I is not, nor ever had been* powerless over alcohol/drugs/whatever, only the conditions into which I is born, I had been powerless over those, but hadn't I made those manageable, even for me?

Fuck this, I sphinx.

'28-DAYS'

'28-DAYS' the neon light flashes again.

Oh fuck 'em then, and I again resolve to fight them with compliance, like a little ickle wormie.

Fleur looks at me, with a twinkle winkle in her peep holes and then reaches into a drawer and brings out a small console, with its very own wand.

'It's the Big Book,' sayz she, passing it to me as though it is the most sacred of all enchiridions.

Shite, I is sphinxing, the effing bible in my palm.

'And a wand for cross-referencing, making notes in the review pane, super isn't it,' she sayz.

I fort she is gonna wet herself with glee. Hee hee.

I takes it from her, sphinxing that I at least could crank up the Phrontistery with my own readings of Job and Ecclesiastes, just like I had in Moss-Side Women's Prison.

'It's the book written by our founding father, Bill W,' sayz she.

'I thought the founding farva is God,' sayz I, now unable to hide the scorn I feel.

'Well, yes, he is too, but through Bill, oh yes, he worked through Bill, and then through Bob and . . . oh dear, I know you're going to come to believe and love so much our fellowship, but you can read the Big Book any time you want, *any time you want* . . .' she sayz.

Yippee, sphinx I. Not even the original big book, but some sorry version scribbled by a man named Bill who had a mate called Bob! I had to piss into a variety of pots (some things never change, eh!) which I won't go into any detail in order to save you, after which Fleur shows me to my own ickle room.

White.

With pink cushions and pink duvet cover. Yuk!

No windows.

Just a ventilation slot at the top of each wall.

She even has to have her irises scanned just to get me in. I am, again, beginning to sphinx this is all one abnormous mistake.

'Now, here are your clothes,' she sayz, and she opens a cupboard to show me several changes of black velour tracksuit type thing.

'Why this?' I asks.

'Well, you all wear black tracksuits because it keeps you all the same, no fashion here you see, we do as much as we can to keep ego out there,' sayz she. 'Now, chop chop, get a shower, then get changed and I'll take your old clothes away and then you can relax a while with your Big Book before Dr. Groome is ready to see you.'

My adrenalin soars at his very name.

There is an en-suite wet room. I haven't had a decent shower for years. I strip off my prison garb and saunter straight under the hot water. I would be quite happy to stay here for the rest of my life. But, after ten minutes, it automatically shuts off.

What a joke.

I have no problem really stepping my body into the black velour tracksuit – it is soft, comfy, and would no doubt be good for kung-fu fighting. I throws myself onto the bed. Harder than it looks. Pink implies soft, doesn't it? Not here. I picks up the console and scrolls down to the contents:

And then it lists a whole load of these 'personal stories' so personal they have felt the need to put them in front of the 'recovering' public.

And then, under 'APPENDICES' it has listed:

Well, my dear sistaz, I am already a yawnin', this is already for the delenda pile. But, I want to arm myself with their weird vocab of the 'heart' so I begin to learn the art of the Bill 'N' Bob technique, aka everything Acknowledged. I click on the arrow to go to the second chapter, Bill's story can wait. 'THERE IS A SOLUTION', well, sphinx I, halle-fuckinglooyah! For that. It said thus:

We, of Bill 'n' Bob, know of millions of men and women who were once just as hopeless as Bill. Nearly all have recovered. They have solved the drink/drugs/whatever problem.

Well, I sphinx, solved, they say, so why the daily compulsory Recovery Hour?

KILL BILL, that's what I say.

And get Bob a job.

But no, I mustn't become too alarmed just yet, **'28-DAYS',**

'28-DAYS'.

We are average people of the world. All sections of the world and many of its occupations are represented, as well as many political, economic, social, and religious backgrounds. We are people who would normally not mix.

They have a fucking regular little Utopia in mind here, don't they, sphinx I. And then I fall into the land of slumber. Better than a sleeping pill. Good old Bill!

4

I wake up facing the beige wall. I realise where
I am. I think of my dream – lovely it is, doing
Kill Bill's all over the show. I stretch out my arms
and wonder when Fleur would perhaps bring me
some food. I turn around and nearly jump out
of my skin, though I is well trained not to show
it.

There, sitting beside my bed, in a big black leather
chair that contrasts well against the whites and
pinks, is Dr. Groome. He still has that rhadaman-
thine-like gaze – his eyes are stock still, trying to
bore a hole into me.

'Oh hello there, you're Dr. Groome, aren't you?'
sayz I in my sweetest Blytonesie voice.

He sayz nowt, my dear sistaz. His arms they are
a-folded.

I stretch my arms out again, as though not a care

in the world. Well, I don't really, do I? Not yet, my dear sistaz, not yet.

But soon, just around the corner. I can feel it in the air.

'I want you to give me ten examples of how you were powerless over those things which gave you trouble in your life, alcohol, drugs, whatever,' sayz he.

'Well now, let's see,' sayz I and begin to massage my chin like a wizened old man, not bothering to sit up for him. I'm not a dog, and I am not going to sit up and beg, but I am going to delight in a few tricks. 'Well, there is one time when I collapsed in the street and woke up not knowing how on earth I got there,' sayz I.

He sayz nothing.

'Then there is a time when I is sick all over the place, yeah, sick here, there and everywhere I is, in the Old Duchess of New York on McColl, do you know it? No, wouldn't have thought so.'

He remains silent.

'Erm, then there is this time, yeah, when I took some capsules, and I had no idea whatsoever what they were, I just wanted a high and, guess what yeah, I woke up in a strange man's bed the next morning with no recollection of anything . . .'

He sayz nothing.

'Then there is another time when I blacked out and found myself in an old woman's house full of dogs, and before I knew it a load of old cozzers, police that is, were beating me up and pushing me into a van.'

He still remains silent.

Then . . .

'ENOUGH!' he shouts.

I keep my composure.

'You are encased by a wall of denial, which I must add is not just a river in Egypt,' sayz he, very quietly so that I has to listen carefully to each and every word as it floats out of his stinking mouth and fades into the air.

'Oh yes, yes, not just a river in Egypt, yes, very funny, have a book of step related gags do you?' I asks, feeling Mount Etna disturbance at these cheapo puns that are far worse than any Jehovah related ones.

'SHUT UP!' orders he.

'OK then Mr. Groome, whatever you say, you're the boss!' That's when he gets up from his chair and, using only one hand, grabs hold of my arm and twists it right round and up my back.

It hurts.

I cannot deny that.

But I say nothing, just let my face become smothered into the pink pillow. Then I feel his breath on my ear, he sayz, 'Now listen, no more of this, no more back chat, it's not your fault, it's part of our condition, but no more, you will listen to me, you will allow us to break down your ego and become as a *little lamb*, am I clear?' he asks.

What could I do?

I gives a poor attempt at a nod of assent. I will have to play it differently, this. He releases my arm and returns to his seat, folding his arms.

'Now,' he sayz, 'I want you to listen while I read to you.'

Oh good! Thinks I. A nice ickle story. He clears his throat and begins, in a Jack-A-Nory voice, reading from his own flashier brushed chrome console:

Who cares to admit complete defeat? Our natural instincts cry out against powerlessness. It is painful to truly acknowledge that *we* have let our conditions distort our minds into such an obsession for destruction.

Only an act of Providence can help us.

He stops and looks up at me. THE GAZE.

I do my best face of powerlessness. It is a kind of mix between a Mona Lisa smile and the saintliness of the Virgin Mary combined with the repentance of Mary Magdalene.

'STOP THAT!' shouts he.

'WHAT?' shouts I back, now bursting the former cloud of conceit.

'I am not going to give up on you! Never! Your

success at this programme has much wider benefits, therefore we cannot allow you to fail, we cannot allow ourselves to fail you, we are going to get to you Alex, we are going to break you until you are broken into a million little pieces, then, we are going to restore you back to a normal, healthy, recovering citizen, with your consent. Or without it.'

And with that admirable little speech he leaves my room. Well, I has to admit, tisn't quite what I had been expecting – fort I could name a few feelings, unleash the crocodiles of the eyes, 'bond' then leave.

What now?

BLOOD? Yeah, *right.*

I'll give them FIRE!

'28-DAYS' '28-DAYS' that's all it needs.

Days. Twenty-bastard-eight of them.

Fleur enters with a tray of food that fares not much better than the prison – but on pink plates. The sight is enough to make me vomit. But I force half of it down whilst she sits in the same chair and reads from the preface to the first edition of the Big Book. Some old codgers ruling from the long cold grave. Nowt new there I hear you say.

We, of the Bill 'N' Bob Technique, are more than ten million men, [and women], recovering from a hopeless and destructive state of mind, body and spirit. To show other destructives precisely how we began our recovery processes and continued on the right path is the main purpose of this text. Many do not understand how sick the alcoholic/addict/whatever really is. Besides, we are sure that OUR recovery methods have advantages for all.

Aaah, so that's their game, I sphinx, to make everyone adhere to this Bill 'N' Bob fingy, this is, the new world order, this will order a new world, a vision for all.

'Isn't that so . . . hopeful, so . . . encouraging?' Fleur asks, like she's just been beatified, although she is only batti-fied.

'Mmm,' I mutters whilst chewing a mouthful of spongey tofu. 'Well, I'm going to leave you with your Big Book. Dr. Groome said your denial is like a thick wall used to keeping out bulldozers, but that shouldn't be too hard a task for us here, don't you worry, we'll save you Alex dear. We will. Now, you read and I'll come and get you first thing in the morning to have your first intensive with Dr. Groome.'

And with that, she leaves me solus.

Whenever the stern self-righteous face of Dr Groome enters and infests my mind, my adrenaline becomes like a tsunami.

Never mind, I sphinx, he thinks my walls are made of brick, when in fact, they are made of steel.

And with that I return to the safety of slumber.

5

Fleur breezes into my room as I am tying my hair back off my face into a tight bun at the side of my head.

'Hello there, good morning to you, and here we have your brekkie,' she sayz, putting down a tray of pink bowls – cereal, milk jug, toast and butter and a cuppa tea. It is a delight of a brekkie, I tell thee, in its simplicity. After I finish it I follow her out of my room, actually, it is a cell, isn't it, I can't get out, ergo, it is a cell.

I follow Fleur down another line of corridors in the opposite direction to that taken when I had entered. I is going, I assume, to see the Doc – the groom. I have to prep myself – call on Etna to behave, to keep my mind my own, which isn't much of a task to be honest, it has always been mine own, unlike Blytons, who are forever used to giving away their minds from the day theyz born – to the state, the teachers, the parents, the relatives, the everyone else except themselves.

But me?

No, there has never been anyone to give it to, so I have kept it like a jewel, Nietzschean in its solitariness.

'RIGHT! COME IN!' booms Dr. Groome.

And Fleur, her hands now shaking somewhat, leaves me in this large, horribly shaded room – another large, black leather chair sits there. On the wall are the TWELVE STEPS and even TWELVE TRADITIONS. I'm sphinxin', twelve is a lucky number round here.

'SIT THERE!' sayz he, pointing to a small chintzy comfy chair.

Don't mind if I do, I sphinx. I tries, though, to keeps my head lower than usual, ugh, I know, it pains me now to even write it.

But he sayz, sitting in his leather chair, and turning to face little old me in the corner, 'and you needn't lower your head, I see you!' My heart trips, it has to be said, I had lowered my head and . . . did this man really have x-ray vizeonie or summat?

'You see me what?' I asks in innocence.

'I see your attempts at humility – pathetic!' sayz he, spitting out the words.

'I'm TRYING!' shouts I, again, another conceit.

'I SEE YOU!' shouts he back.

I could feel poor old Etna not knowing whether to explode or retreat.

'Have you conceded that you are powerless? That your life is unmanageable?' asks he.

'YES!' shouts I.

'LIAR!' Shouts he back in my face.

'FUCK YA THEN!' I shouts now with all sincerity.

'You see, that's where you are, you see, I am writing a book, well, I have written several, all about this societal scourge of addiction. This book is called Eve and the Fermented Apple of Alcoholism, and you will be its most perfect case study,' sayz he.

'REALLY? GOOD FOR YOU! IF YOU WANT TO SEND ME BACK TO THE PRISON, THEN DO IT, THIS IS JUST A POWER GAME!' shouts I.

'Yes. Yes it is – it's just a power game – to *you*,

but to us, it's the difference between life and destruction.'

A slice of silence enters the room and sits betwixt us.

I, my dear sistaz, am in confusion, that is, without fusion. I sphinx he is being a tad melodramatic for starters.

D'ya get me, lah?

Besides, I am not an addict/alcoholic/whatever.

NEVER! You know that, my dear sistaz. I will never be this man's 'case study'.

There had to be someway outta here.

'Who cares to admit COMPLETE DEFEAT? Practically NO ONE . . .' he sez.

I gets up to go. My lug holes have been insulted enough – give me back the years ahead in Moss-Side Women's. . .

He stands in front of me and pushes me back down.

Etna's flames are leaping farva and farva up.

'YOU.

WILL.

STAY.

HERE,' sayz he.

'There's too much resting on your shoulders, on ours, and we WILL NOT FAIL!'

I fold my arms and let them rest with the bajulation of the muvva they had always to carry. I switch on my Phrontistery to run in the background. I put on a soundtrack – Eminem – and then imagine me and the Grrrlz gliding down Oxford Road, in our balletics and mechanics – kung-fu fighting as the mood takes us – that, my dear sistaz, now seems like Utopia.

'Only an act of Providence can remove it from us . . .' he continues, the words breaking into my dreams, my other ontological landscapes. He is like a deranged Texan Born Again Christian. 'We perceive that only through utter defeat are we able to take our first steps toward liberation and strength . . .'

Me and the Grrrlz are still gladly gliding past the MRI, tormenting the Blyton drip behind the bar of the Old Duchess of New York . . . and so, this went on for most of the day, my first of the twenty-eight, **'28-DAYS' '28-DAYS' '28-DAYS'**. But, I has to confess, my dearest of dear sistaz, I feel a bit down in the old dumpsteroonies.

'Should this week go ok you should be able to join a group next week,' Fleur sayz, bringing in my tray of din dins which turns my stummick just to look at. I want my bed – my slumber – my Phrontistery. I don't want to begin to even sphinx about what delights tomorrow holds in store for me, and so, as I force a few mouthfuls down my neck and Fleur begins to read from the blasted Big Book I throw myself on the bed and let my mind wander to the Good Old Days – the only God I ever had and/or needed. The days of teasing those of the Piccashitty Palare, the meatheads, the dum dums, our muvva fukkas, the drip behind the bar, the old Gutshot Rebos!

There, isn't that a JOKE!

That me and the Grrrlz had spent our free time in a health affirmative bar, drinking wheatgrass with daggers?

This, dear sistaz, only confirmed to me that these damned people know naught of what they speak, Dr. Groome can't see beyond his own finger, never mind to see what I IS!

6

It is the next morning and I awake with a heavier
heart than usual – I'm not chattin' 'bout a heart
that is, like, fired up with the old angria, but the
heart that is, like, stuck in pot of treacle – heavy,
sticky . . . Anywayz, I has a quick chat with meself,
call on Etna to back me up. But now she is beginning to behave a bit like a drunken old woman
– tired, and staggering.

'COME ON!' I ROAR

and thus I successfully kicks the flame into action
– for she sends me a flame back to reach up and
kiss me on the cheek. And so I follows dear old
Fleur, the faded flower, out of the cell and once
more onto the runway that leads up to the groom's
power base.

'Come on in then, take your seat,' sayz he, already
ready and waiting for me from his big leather seat,

his arms folded, his mouth grim. His gaze follows me:

> from the door
>> across the floor
>>> past him and to
>>>> 'my' flowery chintzy seat.

'27 DAYS'

'27 DAYS'

We sit in silence for a good five mins or so.

He's such a power hungry prick.

'So. How was your sleep last night?' he asks, with a smirk attempting to hide in the corner of his mouth.

'It was ok,' I lied.

'OK?'

'Yeah! OK!'

'Well, it's a new day, yesterday's history, tomorrow's a mystery,' sayz he.

This guy is really sick, d'ya get me, lah?

'That's why it's called the present – it's a gift.'

Well, sphinx I, hurry up and get me through this, then you can stick the gift up your arse.

'Little good can come to an alcoholic/addict/ whatever UNLESS! . . . she has first accepted her devastating weakness and ALL its consequences.'

He stops.

Hallie-fuckedoff-yoola! I nods.

'So, what drugs?' he asks.

'None,' replies I.

'Moss-Side girl like you, no drugs? Pull the other one, it's got bells on.'

I thought he said he saw me – this pretender.

'Alcohol then, yes, you're a drinker alright,' sayz he.

'Yes, drinker, that is me,' sez I. I don't sphinx telling him any different would serve any purpose whatever, even though I'd not so much as taken a sip of alchie-hol – ever.

'Until you humble yourself, your sobriety, IF ANY! Will be PRECARIOUS!'

I nods again.

'Of REAL HAPPINESS – she will find NONE!' another noddie for this old noddie. 'SELF-confidence is no good! No good at all – ESPECIALLY where alcohol/drugs/whatever are concerned, do you understand?'

I nods again.

'YOU!

ALEXANDRA!

ARE!

A!

LIAR!'

shouts he, right in front of me face.

'Yeah, ok, so I am,' sayz I. I'm having too much of all this palava.

'So! This wall of denial is stronger than we previously though, mmm?' asks he.

'Yes, obviously,' replies I.

'When was your last drug/drink/whatever?' he asks.

'Drug? Never.

Drink? Never so much as a sip.

Whatever? Well, whatever.'

'Aah, I get it – yes! It's the biggest one of the lot isn't it, I know YOU!' he sayz, now like an electrified evangelical minister, 'YOU! ARE! ADDICTED! TO!

ADRENALIN!'

Well, what could I say? He isn't far off the mark, but then, I just see adrenaline as a by-product of anger and rage.

WHAT.

EVVER.

'YOU! ARE! THE! VICTIM! OF! A! MENTAL OBSESSION! IT IS SO POWERFUL THAT NO! HUMAN WILL CAN FIX IT! Am I making myself clear?'

I nod.

But, dear sistaz, I has to tell you, I is now getting, well, not scared as such, but a tad fearful for my sanity here, these people, well, theyz totally off the planet altogether, d'ya get me, and I want nothing more to do wiv 'em.

I! WANT! OUT!

And so, I gets up from my chair, stands in front of him and shouts, OUT! OUT! OUT!

He then grabs hold of my arm and attempts to push me against the wall. I lift a knee. But, dear sistaz, it seems like I misjudged this geezer, he sees it coming and quickly steps to the side. Well, I am all fired up now, aren't I, yes, of course, it is my addiction to adrenalin! Or whatever. I launch my fist into his ribs. Seems like he can do a few of his own moves too. But, dear sistaz, whilst I pride myself on taking on any man – two, I cannot do, not unless theyz particularly drippy. You see, this is the point at which Clive walks in and grabs me from behind. I can smell geography teacher all over him. It is just truly sickening. Anyway, they has me on the floor, face down. Just like they used to do in my early days in prison – and last day – hee hee haw haw.

Well, within minutes they have locked me back into my cell. Me, shouting all the way, that I is **NEVER** going to conform to their idiotic plans for world domination with the help of the flowerpot men or this ridiculous notion of Eve and the Fermented Apple of Alcoholism. This girl is not ready, NEVER would be, for joining the docile herds. Old Groomey man shouts that I will be, in his word, GROOMED to join the herd of recovery, that I have been sat at the bottom of a well for long enough. Well!

I demand to be allowed to return to prison. They tell me I no longer own any choice. This, they say, is my rock bottom, and that it is part of the Process™, and with providential strength invested in them, they will save me FROM MYSELF! That they will get me to the point where I can perform my own INSIDE JOB!

INSIDE JOB! Etna is having a ball of a time now – from allowing her flame to reduce somewhat yesterday she is now back stronger than ever. These people are not at all into strictures of structures, but strictures of people's interiors.

I needn't tell you that it goes against everything I stand for.

YES! STAND FOR!

Am I not a product of my earliest environment?

Or is it a mere co-incidence that they had to build a prison especially for MOSS-SIDE WOMEN? Because it just so happened that MOSS-SIDE WOMEN are all born BAD/SICK/WHATEVER? It is the old triangle – structuralism/existentialism/post-structuralism, and now, RECOVERY!!

So called 'recovery'.

The grand narratives are far grander than any previously experienced and they aren't plural either, this narrative is grand, and singular – the 12-STEPS! The only H.P. in town. And then, I knew it had to be mentioned sooner, rather than later. The old H.P. - - BUT! Not my own dream factory – but their H.P. – the old grey bearded one himself, the finger pointing cloud dweller of the O.T.

'It is a statistical fact that NO ALCOHOLIC/ADDICT/WHATEVER EVER! EVER! Recovers on their OWN resources – therefore we must seek

out one who can be ALL LOVING, ALL GUIDING
– let us turn to HIM now!'

Well, my dear sistaz, I has to ask meself where
I is, because this is THE muvvafukkin dystopias of
ALL! Dystoptias.

'HOLD ON ONE LITTLE MINUTE HERE!
What did you say?' asks I.

He went to repeat the whole shebang.

I hold my hand in the air to stop him – like an
old fashioned air traffic controller.

'WHOA THERE – DID I HEAR YOU SAY
'HIM'?' I hold the word in the air like a duchess
with something the dog dragged in between her
white silk covered fingers.

'YES! It's just a word, Him, as YOU understand
HIM!' sayz he, his eyes now twitching as I had
backed him into the corner.

'Well, I don't understand HIM, nor will I ever
– have you ever been to Moss-Side?' asks I now in
all seriousness.

'We drove through it once – I saw all I needed
to see – I didn't grow up too far from a bad area
you know – where I am today, I got to because I
worked hard, and on myself – and now, with the
help of the Bill 'N' Bob Technique we're gonna

clean others up, in those areas – the people will be cleaned up – from the INSIDE!' sayz he.

'With the help of a Him?' asks I. 'Woman has no past, no history, no religion of their own . . . and you deem yourself qualified to TALK. TO. ME!

'ABOUT GOD?!'

I roar.

'This is just another example of your be-llig-er-ence, your denial, hooking itself onto anything at all, it's just a word – we've used it since the dawn of time.'

'Yeah, YOUR TIME, NOT OURS!

YOUR WORDS. NOT OURS.

YOUR HISTORY. NOT OURS.

Well, it hasn't fucking worked for US – HAS IT, YOU FUCKING FUCK WIT BASTARD!' sayz I, and I continue . . . 'and, if you'd been in Moss-Side long enough you'd know that it is *sans* men! The only He I hold any faith in is THE greatest, most misinterpreted one ever – the one whose *scientific* philosophy is as WITHOUT, so WITHIN! Yours is as WITHIN, so WITHOUT – WITHOUT. BEING. THE. OPERATIVE. WORD!' I stop.

His eyes are twitching even more.

He has his right hand clenched into a fist.

Hee haw. Hee haw.

'Aaaahh! So. You're a READER?!' he throws it at me.

I catches it.

'Exactamondo!' sayz I.

'So, you are our perfect little Eve after all - and tell me, where do you get your material?' asks he.

'Well, I have a Blyton friend who borrowed me her irises to get into central centre of the written word, innit.'

'Who is this Blyton to whom you refer?' asks he.

'Now, that would be tellin' wouldn't it, eh?' Dear sistaz, I is, of course, lying my little head off – no Blyton would do such a thing – not even Mid, an ex-Blyton, would let a Moss-Sider into the inner sanctum. That Mid is a total fuck up, aye, that she is. Middling Mid. Groome seems to have no idea of the tiny blue light district on Tib Street.

He orders me to be taken back to my cell.

And so I am.

Fleur is in all of a dither.

'Oh dear, dear Alexandra, what have you done

to yourself? You've made your position in life so much more difficult . . . don't you want a second chance, mmm?' she asks.

'Listen Fleur,' sayz I, 'I never even had a first one, d'ya get me?'

'Now now, I know what you're saying, really I do, but self-pity is a character defect. You'll hopefully learn that when you come to do step four, that is, we take a fearless moral inventory of ourselves using fourteen character defects as our guide, based on the seven deadly sins. . .' sayz she, and pats my hand, like it's the head of a Schitzu yapping bag dog.

'SELF-PITY?' asks me.

'HOW. ON. EARTH. IS IT SELF-PITY?'

'Well, now, it's not for us to question, of course Jesus Christ himself, well, he is a bit of a rebel, but, well, try and put the debating society on hold . . .'

'FUCK. YOU. FLEUR. YOU. FUCKING. OLD. FADED. FUCK.' There is no danger of my impressing people with my vocabulary range, eh? But, my point had always been just that. To make a point. Nice and sharp. And properly punctuated. And only a good FUCK could do that, especially when it fell on the ears of the Blytons. 'But that's how you lot have always worked, innit, now using these character defects, based on YOUR morals, which you change from time to time whenever it suits you, then impose as devices of shame on US! To say what it is like, with even a hint of pathos – that's self-pity, is it?' I asks.

'Now listen, there's a time for everything – you will be able to explore your feelings more when . . .'

'WHEN I'VE FIRST CRUCIFIED MYSELF? I'LL BE ABLE TO RISE FROM THE DEAD TO INDULGE IN OMPHALEOSKEPSIS ON SOME OVERPAID SHRINK'S COUCH?'

'Oh dear, well, I suggest you read some of the Big Book whilst we're waiting for Dr. Groome to decide what he's going to do with you – he isn't one for giving up, no, never, only switching tactics. You have the power to make it easier on yourself Alex dear.'

'But he said it is a condition which I had NO control over, what's it to be?' asks I.

'Now now ENOUGH!' Fleur said. Her hands are shaking. Poor old mare. I am rattling a cage she doesn't know she's been in.

She leaves me alone and I sit on the floor and do the old Star Rover bit – that is, I propel myself on a journey into my Phrontistery. It is like this: Me, of course, dancing, ballet, hippy-hop, all the way down Oxford Street, jumping over the heads of the meekly studious Blytons who are only there because it is part of their pre-defined journey. And then it is into the old Holy Name church where I'd leap over the pews and dance on the altar – on the altar of Alex! Where I belong, still. What I have learned here, thus far, is that it is better to beat oneself up, to divorce the most authentic bit of me for their most moral and conventional presentation, than to beat up the system. !!!!FUCK!!!!

7

Dearest of dear sistaz, I can not believe what these people are saying. It is, in a word from their own language, an 'OUTRAGE'.

I have now **'26 DAYS'** to go. And, whilst I remind myself I don't even want to be here no more, the prospect of release is also too good to ignore.

Dr. Groome enters my cell. Fleur's head is bowed, like a Geisha, and off she trundles – away! Away! Groome sits on the edge of my bed and rests his hands on his knees. He has obviously been to great lengths to show me how understanding, how *gentle* he can be. Tosser.

'Well, Alex, it wasn't to be until next week that you were to join one of the groups, but I think it may help you come to understand the nature of denial, and you will have the *privilege* of listening to other alcoholics/addicts/whatever's *experience, strength and hope.'* He now stares at me to gauge how I have taken this tripe that has left his mouth.

'Oh Good! I'm *sooooo* pleased,' sayz I, with a glint in my eye.

'I'm going to ignore your sarcasm, it's just another strand of your anger, your self-centredness . . . *your FEAR.'*

I laffs in a high pitch.

'FEAR?' I repeats back to him.

'Yes, fear, you're really nothing but a scared, lost little girl, a scared alcoholic/addict/whatever.'

I almost fall off the opposite edge of the bed. That's when he grabs my arm, or rather, that's when I allow him to grab my arm and push me out of the door,

back down the corridor,

past his office,

down past other white mysterious doors and then into a lift,

up two floors

and through another white door and then,

into a larger room.

I notice the one-way mirror the minute we enter. There are half a dozen other people, I guess they are alcoholics/addicts/whatevers, just from the way their shoulders, like Fleur's, are hunched over. One is shaking. Not from fear. But. From anger. I recognize it straight away. He holds himself and stares at the floor, as though that is where the enemy is. Another has tears running down his face. Aaah, he wanted his mummykins, sphinx I, but then he looks up at me, this new arrival and my scathing face, and his mirrored mine, and then becomes vicious, spiteful, and the look he throws me might as well have been a mouthful. This group is led by the man and woman who had both been in the foyer the day I had been 'admitted', the day they thought I'd be doing the admitting – hee hee haw haw. Ula and Clive.

Ula gets up and walks over to me and Groome. I am rather pushed and poked to sit down at an empty seat. Seems theyz been expecting me. Ula 'tells' everyone to introduce themselves to me. 'This,' she tells me, once Groome leaves the room, 'is the newcomers meeting, the step one meeting . . .'

'Oh good, well, I'll just sit here and observe then, shall I,' I replies.

The angry man who I saw first looks up and, like a schoolboy, giggles.

'SHUT UP TIM!' cries Ula.

The whip has descended.

Each member in turn is then told to 'share' with me their name and five minutes of ESH – that is, Experience, Strength and Hope. I lift my head to the ceiling and listen.

Wot else can I do?

'Hello, my name's Gina, I'm an alcoholic/addict/ whatever. Well, I first realised I had a problem when I had my second blackout. I just thought the first one was a fluke, but the second time it happened, well, I woke up in a man's bed – I didn't even know his first name, never mind his second . . .'

I nearly fall off my chair with laughter. Tim giggles again.

'SHUT IT,' Ula tells me! And then, rather schizo like, urges Gina on with an attempt at a kind, caring, understanding voice.

'That's when I knew I must be an alcoholic/ addict/whatever, I also have issues around men, and relationships,' she sayz. She blah blahs on. Then it is Tim's turn:

'My name's Tim and I'm an alcoholic/addict/ whatever. I'd always wanted to stop drinking and doing coke and whatever, but could never do it on me own, I drunk like a pig, I did, well, they say if you want to know why you drink, stop drinking and you'll find out, well, I did, and I'm just beginning to realise, I'm also realising that everything I am I'm also the equal opposite and that there's no mummy and daddy that's gonna come and rescue me, not that there ever fucking was to begin with . . .' then he giggles, then cries. Then it is James's turn:

'I was a binge drinker, occasional coke user, can't see how that's made me into a fucking alcoholic/addict/ whatever though, I have a formidable reputation in my industry you know, everyone in my industry sayz I make good morning sound like a declaration of war, I AM SOMEBODY! I do NOT belong here – FUCK YOU ALL!' he sayz and then gets up, picks up his chair and throws it across the hall. Then he sits down on the floor and cries like a baby.

I claps like a child at the circus. Then it is Nick's turn.

My name's Nick, and I haven't yet decided whether I'm an alchie . . . I think this is just a big power trip on the part of the state and it's fucked up kunting institutions, Foucault said . . .' Ula stood up.

'Yes Nick, we've heard it all before, FUCK FOUCAULT! Gina, can you repeat, for the sake of his die-hard fan, which only goes to show how sick he really is, what Foucault's problem is?'

Gina looks keen and eager to give teacher the apple.

'Yes, Foucault was most definitely a sex addict, and more besides,' she announces.

'And what does that mean, Gina?' Ula asks, tip tapping her Fuck Me heels on the floor, her arms folded.

'It meanz that his theories and thoughts, that is, his whole works, should be ignored, the works and thoughts of an alcoholic/addict/whatever are unsound – they have come from an unsound mind.'

'Well done Gina, tomorrow you'll be going into the step 2 group,' Ula sayz.

Gina looks like she is going to wet herself.

My dear sistaz, I could not believe the mumpsimus I had just heard. It is the nightmare of all nightmares and the only way to dispel nightmares is to fucking well get stuck right in. D'ya get me, lah?

'That's OUTRAGEOUS!' shouts I in my best Blyton.

'Oh really?' Ula asks.

'Yes. Really! What about one of the three greatest thinkers of last century?' I asks.

'Which one?' she asks, boring her daggered eyes into me. Or trying.

'You mean the prole lover?' she asks, and then sneers. Gina copies.

Little bitch. She is now on my 'to get' list.

'He, your beloved prole lover, was an alcoholic, that renders all of what he said and wrote NULL. AND. VOID! On the other hand, Freud remains valid!' she sayz, continuing to tip tap her Fuck Me heels around the circle.

'Well, I rather think you has that the wrong way round entirely,' sayz I.

'How so?' she asks.

'Well, the one you deem worthy had Phallus as King, for both men and women – the other wanted equality,' sayz I.

Gina looks scared and looks first at me, then up at Ula.

'I see you!' Ula shouts and lowers her face so that it is almost touching mine.

'Ula Sees? Does she? Then what about James Joyce? Is he not worthy? Charles Dickens the workaholic? Jean Rhys, Richard Yates, Raymond Carver . . .'

'Shut up you stupid little girl,' she sayz.

Well, I'd just about had it with this tregateur. I jumps up and aim a sharp kung-fu kick at her back.

Down she goes.

Tim and James hold their hands over their mouths. That is their problem – all whinge and no action. Gina jumps up on top of her chair and, like a distressed chimp, begins making weird noises. Within seconds, with miss Fuck Me lay out cold on the floor I am grabbed. I had forgotten about quiet Clive in a dark, far corner of the room. I began to give it to him too. But then Groome enters and within seconds I have been stabbed in the arm and am out like a light.

They couldn't even fight.

PART THREE

1

For two whole days I have been kept in a worser worserer cell than that which Moss-Side Women's could ever dream up. On the wall a moving picture of a young woman, a maid, I believe they used to call them, anyway, this pilgarlick is giving me what I suppose is a lesson in humility and subservience. I is stuck in a chair, literally, by beams of light that stun me if I move more than an inch in any direction. I have to watch. This is interweaved with on the hour meetings from, you guessed it, The Recovery Channel.

And, yeah, get this, they even have docudrama fings in which these failed actors pretend theyz Foucault, Nietzsche, Marx *et al* and they are then interrogated in the court of historical accuracy – presided over by an expert panel. That's when I come face to face with more of me own history.

For, who should walk through the door but our bass-voice of Cheshire, complete with his scarlet letter.

He sees me and nods his head slowly, his eyes narrowed. I can't deny it. My heart, yes, I do have one, it sinks at the sight of this man whilst I is welded, almost, to this poxy chair.

'This is the one, it is SHE! Her and a group of the OTHERS! They were the ones who abolished the serenity of our Serenity and attacked us – right in our own idyll!' cries he to Dr. Groome.

Dr. Groome seems to relish this new bit of info.

'There's no doubt that she is a chronic alcoholic/ addict/whatever – she proves beyond doubt that, whilst the alcohol might be in the bottle, the ISM's are in HER!' sayz he. They both nod their heads now.

'BUT!' sayz Groome, his eyes shining, 'she would be my GREATEST case study, would she not, perfect for Eve and The Fermented Apple of Alcoholism?'

Bass-voice/Scarlet letter's eyes twinkle, contrast quite well with the redness of the I!

I had already guessed pecuniary advantage in this somewhere.

These places, the Recovery Channel, theyz not charities you know. Anyways, he sits opposite me and reiterates what Groome has already said, 'We are going to save you, little Eve, bitten the apple of knowledge, but you didn't know it had fermented, did you?'

'And this kind man here is our centre's greatest investor,' explains Groome.

'FUCK.

OFF.' I shouts back.

'Well, we have twenty-four days left . . .'

That's when it hits me, like a bolt of lightening from the invisible God man,

'24-DAYS',

the light flashes on and off, like the knickers of a plastic tit whore.

I can do this.

Can't I?

And by resting very heavily on the sins of the mother, surely?

I would just pretend to be my muvva – inhabit

her greasy, saddo little world for the next twenty-four days. I would be the Seanachai exemplar.

Anyway, that's how it begins – The Compromise. I fall into method and lower my head an inch, and feel a state that could only be described as savage.

It is empathy, I think.

She is still a fuckin' fucked up muvvafukka, don't let's get that wrong. But now, well, she is a part of me.

'I . . . I . . . I'm sorry, I think, I think I've reached rock . . . bottom . . . at least, it feels like that,' I sayz and, out of nowhere, comes a Niagara falls from me peepholes. I can see the faces of both men soften immediately.

They can now be secure in their power.

And my seeming lack of it.

I is conforming to my sex.

Hee haw hee haw.

'Switch the laser beams off,' Groom shouts.

And as soon as theyz switched off I lift my knees up to my chest and sob like a bambino.

'There there now, you're in a safe place,' sayz Groome and puts his arms around my shaking shoulders.

'This is dynamite!' Mr Clockwork Apple sez.

'We'll have to get her on Recovery Channel as soon as she's gone through the steps – a beacon of light to other Moss-Siders, eh?' He's almost pissing himself with excitement.

'I'm broken,' sayz I, ladling it on for x-tra f-ekt.

'Good, that's good, now, I want you to 'share' with us ten examples of your powerlessness over alcohol,' sayz he, his eyes like stars.

'Well, ooh, I dunno, it's hard this, but, well, I is always, like, wetting up the furniture, the sofa, and then wondering how that had happened,' I begin.

It felt quite easy once I'd taken on the body of dear old Muvva. Actually, I is beginning to feel a tad, erm, sympathetic towards the old muvva fukka. They did say it is an illness, a condition, even an *allergy*.

But anyway, ons I goes, listing the remainding nine. Then they sayz, 'now, that's good, well done, very well done, you needn't drink again, but what we want to know now is, can you list ten examples of how your life had become unmanageable?' he asks.

Mr. Fermented Apple pushes forward on his chair, and leans in closer.

'Well, I wouldn't get up for the day-centre, you know, where they learn us pottery and that, and I would just stay home and . . .' I falter.

'Yes, go on, it's ok, we're listening.'

'Read!' sayz I.

Both men take sharp inward breaths.

'What did you read on your own?' sayz Mr. Apple.

'Nietzsche, Hegel . . . Marx,' sayz I, tears racing down my cheeks. Both men hold their hands over their mouths.

'And . . . de Beauvoir, Mitchell, Kristeva . . .' Dr. Groome gets up and begins to pace the room, and even run his hands through his hair. Yare.

'I knew it is wrong, but, but, I is *desperate*, I couldn't stop drinking, drugging, whatever, and I is looking for *answers*,' sayz I.

'Yes, yes, of course you are, there there now, it's ok, you're ok now,' Mr. Apple sayz.

By the end of the following week, with only '**14 DAYS**' to go I am in the step four group. I have spent several days in each of the step one, two and three groups. I have acknowledged that I have been corrupted by alcohol/drugs/whatever and that I had been unmanageable. I have acknowledged that The Group could help me conform to Sanity™. And I have decided to turn myself to The Group, its Will and Sanity™ and H.P. as we knew Him. My dear sistaz, it *is* a Him!

But never mind, under the mask of muvva I surrender whilst protecting who I really is. It's called integrity. Or in- too- gritty, for that is from whence we came. And it is way too gritty for some that theyz deny the very concept at every turn lest theyz have to confront it in themselves.

And now, in the step four group with Clive and Ula (Ula! Ula Sees bugga all) I am to make 'a fearless inventory of the filth my life had become/ always is . . .'

But first we have to sit and listen to one of the lead actors on the Recovery Channel read, from autocue, step four. I listen intently.

Fail to prepare. Prepare to fail an' all that.

I watch. And listen. And, what it comes down to is that it's about instincts gone awry. Oh but, they do concede that some of our instincts are 'ok' – but only in moderation – balance, yin and yang.

Sex is good – but too much salt is bad for you

[dehydration?] – and too much pepper would make you sneeze. Ambition is also a healthy thing, apparently, but only if you first accept where you are in life and see any work as 'service', especially to the nice boss who happens to take you on and who happens also to be a Blyton. And then it goes on and on about how we hurt others, we step on their toes and theyz can't help but kick us back even harder in return. But it is we that are to blame. We wuz gonna have to make things right with them – but not to think about that just now, cos we are on step four, not step eight or nine, the mention of which always has James in tears and Gina straining at the leash – paffetik guilt bag that she is. But one question does rear its head – what would it be like to have me own muvva actually conforming to this Bill 'N' Bob technique? It would stop her pissin' up the sofa after the nightly visit to the old Duchess of New York on McColl that's for sure – but would it make her a better muvva?

Would it have made her a better muvva?

Would my life have been different had she been

'forced' to embrace Bill 'N' Bob before, or since, I had been born?

Should they force drinking muvvas to be to accept Recovery?

OK, so it is more than one question, which shows how much my Phrontistery has been busy whirring away with itself, off the beaten track of the sacred dream factory. Well, it is a dream, of sorts, is it not? And, like most dreams, is unlikely to become reality.

Anyway! Didn't fuckin' matter no more wevver my old mumsy ever got step one.

What would I do should I manage to hold onto this until I is released? There.

That is the ONE question worth asking.

The actor's voice had droned on and on, but still I listened, as an alkie, junkie, whatevver! We are told that we will be confessing, err, 'sharing' our step four peccavihs punctatim, which will then become step five punctatim, with either Ula if you are a girly wirly, or Clive if you are a boy ahoy!

It is to be my step five day first – Gina is almost crying. This is, apparently, the Bar Mitzvah of the programme. Yeah!

It is the morning of the day of my step five peccavih. Fleur enters my room, hands still shaking and, whilst I eat my porridge – full of oats, good for the nervous system, she sayz, which, I thought, mustn't have done her much good, she sits and reads to me from step five. It is all about sharing and, if one wanted, one could go to a church and read it to a minister of some sort, or a Bill 'N' Bob Technique approved counsellor or whatever. But I have no choice. It is Ula or nowt. I don't mind. Isn't as if the step 4/5 is even mine.

Then a fort occurs to me, I am doing this on behalf of my dear old mumsy – aaahhhh, coz she hadn't been able to do it herself.

I don't stay on *THAT* track for long.

Anyhoo . . . Dr. Groome enters my cell just as Fleur is taking my breakfast tray back out. He hands me a round chip – plastic it is, like a casino chip. But he wants a diamond reaction in return. I looks down at it. My eyes fill up. On the back it sayz:

'*To thine ownself be true*'.

Hee hee haw haw.

Hadn't I been true to myself before this lousy

episode in my life?

Hadn't it been true to make my misery of a life a work of art and not fall into the disadvantaged herds? Anyways, the tears, they did run down. And, like an American day-time soap I squeeze the chip within my hand and whisper, 'Thank you. So much.'

'It's my pleasure,' sayz he.

Aaaahhhh. A digi-moment.

He escorts me to a small room that has two chintzy big softy chairs, at the side of which is a small coffee table with, guess what, a box of peach coloured tissues. This, apparently, is the step five peccavih room. I bow my head and, as Groome leaves, Ula enters. It is 9.30am.

By 2pm I have 'bravely shared' 'my' step five peccavih with Ula 'sees nowt'. We even have a hug and she sayz to me, 'this meanz that so many women from Moss-Side Women's Prison will be able to have a second chance, with the help of this pro-gramme.' I nod my head and cries some more – this bonding moment – me and Ula – crying on behalf of all the ravaged women everywhere!

I am then allowed to watch an old film in my

cell. A classic they call it. It is called, guess what, **'28-DAYS'**, with some old actress called something bollocks.

It makes me nearly want to vomit. But, as the horse makes its appearance, something about Blyton equine therapy (purrleezze!), I provides the obligatory Blyton-esque tears.

It is, Dr. Groome informs me, no time to become complacent, for step six is a-waiting.

The next morning Fleur comes in and, whilst I munch on muesli, she keeps going on and on about how this step separates the 'men from the boys' . . . mmm.

It is 'I'm willing to align myself to the Sanity™ of the Group and thus remove all the filth I had been contaminated with,' the filth which I have discovered in my steps four and five peccavihs. I has got them all. Jealousy. Envy. Intolerance. Impatience. Vanity. Self-centredness. Dishonesty. Self-pity. Etcetera. Etcetera. Etcetera. The ones that keep on repeating themselves, though, are self-pity and 'emotional' dishonesty. Or rather, they are my muvva's. I have, at last, been able to take her inventory *and* have it validated – granted, not as hers, but hey, my head knows. Ula and I 'share' with each other, and with the Group about step six.

Gina shares how glad she is that she has connected with her feelings and is now ready to walk the way of the Woman.

(Hee hee whore whore!)

Me? I shares that I am now ready to 'With Humility™ serve and obey The Group and thus Society' and I lay great emphasis on the 'humility doesn't equal humiliation aspect' – yeah, right!

And, sailing smoothly through steps six and seven we arrive at step eight – 'Made a list of persons whose feet we had stamped on even if theyz kicked us back dead hard . . .' type thingy.

PHEW!

So, now, who had my dear old mumsy hurt the most?

You got it!

Moi!

So, in my muvva's best whingey voice, I sayz to myself, 'Alex, I want you to know how very vewwwy sowwwwy I am, truly, for making you and then delivering you into such a world and then for not giving so much as a shite about you, I shall live in purdah for the rest of my days . . .' Hee haw hee haw.

So, folks, I make a list, my muvva's list – I name

the Drip behind the bar of the old Duchess of New York, for my muvva has been a pain in the arse there every night – and probably still is. I also put down all the neighbours, and anyone else she could possibly have come into contact with.

Then, I am told, step nine beckons. I am now to 'Acknowledge and rectify those harms discovered thus far'. I also has to put down the old bass-voice/scarlet letter, and the headmistress of the Mrs. Gaskell Academy for Girls. The ones *they* know about – otherwise they'd get wondering. It is then 'suggested' to me, they always underline and bold 'suggested . . . it's just a suggestion but . . .' it is just like 'God, Him, but as you understand Him', that I make my first amend – that is, to write a letter to Mrs. Gaskell's headmistress.

Anyways, I has to do this letter – which isn't really a letter – no one is trusted with pens anymore – which meanz my sitting in a room with a camera fixed on my sorry face and then I tell her 'how very sowwwy' I am, even though it is her own fault she she can only preach kindness to her 'girls' but wouldn't practice it by opening the poxy door. Then I has to do another one for the deaded dum dum – whom, it has to be pointed out, stood on my toes

FIRST and who, by rights, should have done their own bloody peccavihs and then amends to me . . . calm down Alex. I am calm.

You *see?*

Then I am assured that I would just be on the path of making amends when, and if, I leave.

It is nearing now, dear sistaz.

Nearing now.

Then I am elevated – or 'fast tracked' into the step ten group – only Gina is in there – James and Tim and co are all stuck behind in step whatever. Still trying to work out how to best manage their impressions to suit Clive and Ula, whereas they couldn't do that, because they really are alcoholics/addicts/whatever, and because theyz also wanted to be Blytons more than anything else.

Anyway, step ten is all about keeping constant watch on yourself every minute of every single day, which meanz that if, like Gina, you are a tad predisposed to guilt and beating oneself with a big stick, then this would enable that process. It also fosters constant questioning of self, so that you can't relax at all, especially when in contact with others. You have to say things like 'boundaries' and 'resentment' and 'sorry, so so sorryyyyyy' and chalk up your 'sins' at the end of each day.

What a jolly!

It is day twenty-five.

My dear sistaz, I have been here for three weeks and four days.

Oh, how time flies when you're having fun.

I am moved up into Step eleven Group – which meanz I have to practice talking to an invisible He-God and, get this, then listen to see if He replies.

I would rather have read Grimm's Fairy Tales – because there is very little difference.

But, tonight, for the first time, as Fleur escorts me back to my cell with a cup of hot chocca for her good girly wurly, I get down on my knees, join my hands together and close my eyes, then, like a kiddy winky, I pray. It is, dear sistaz, like believing in Santa Claus all over again – not that I ever did, but it is a most appropriate analogy. It is also great for mental health issues – for what it does is have me direct my hopes, fears and what not to this invisible not-earthly thing, so that, whenever fings went wrong on our earthly plane I could just ask this invisible 'He' for help in accepting all those fings I cannot change – like Moss-Side for starters, and to change the fings I can – which is mainly all the bad stuff I have been constantly told I carry within my being. So the character defects are my own, but the good things, well, theyz given from God, so I isn't to take any personal credit for those.

Oh no, that just would not do.

What it meanz is that I have my head in this invisible 'spiritual' plane and my body walking the earth, or rather, *working* the earth.

God would help me accept this Bitch of a life.

'Aaahhh, you're recovering so well,' Fleur sayz, her hands wibbly wobbling all over the show. She sits down on the edge of my bed and looks over me, like I supposed a fairy tale muvva would to her beloved daughter.

'Fleur,' sayz I, 'were you in here too?' asks I. She nods her head. 'Yes, eight years ago, that's how long I've been 'well',' sayz she.

'So why do your hands shake all the time? Are you scared?' asks I, genuinely interested.

'It's fear my dear, fear is at the root of all of our character defects. You know, there are only two emotions in the world – fear and love. I pray and pray and, well, I s'pose I just learn to accept myself just as I am, and accept that it's all for a greater purpose,' she sayz.

Now, you may wonder what had happened to my dear old 'real' mother, Mount Etna within. Well, now she makes herself known – knocks with her flames on the side of my stomach, and reaches up to my heart. It is as if she is saying, WAKE UP! WAKE UP! FIRE! FIRE! Yes, dear old Alex the authentic is getting very impatient at having to be repressed to make way for this muvva recovery mascaron. And now her calls are stronger than ever.

'Why couldn't you accept yourself the way you were before?' asks I, trying to keep my voice moderated in line with my new found happy joyous and free serenity!

'Well I is killing meself dear, what wiv the alcohol/drugs/whatever . . .' she sayz, her voice up and down.

'But Fleur, I'm sure God will understand if you don't pray for a few days, give yourself some time off from checking in, He won't mind, will he? What do you have to lose?' asks I.

Fleur's hands are now shaking more and more.

'But I've always done it like this – always followed

the programme . . .' she sayz.

I have sown the seed, dear sistaz, I can see she has begun to sphinx about it, this possibility of personal responsibility for self-expression and authenticity and not to being a slave to yet another grand narrative, but that this one is invisible and mean and makes you fucking paranoid that you're being watched all the time.

'Now now, you must get a good night's sleep, you're to be put into step twelve group tomorrow. You've only got two days left, and then, the day after tomorrow they have to do some recordings for the Minister and he'll need to sign your discharge forms. I'm sure you're going to be released on day 28!' she sayz, and then pats me on the head a coupla times, like I's some cute puppy and leaves me alone, on my knees.

'It's hard to stumble when you're on your knees,' she sayz as she leaves.

2

Step twelve is 'Having conformed to Sanity™ and Humility™ as outlined in the Programme of Recovery we live by these Principles™ in every area of our selves and convey this message to others who were contaminated as we once were (which we should never ever forget).'

Tall order, eh!

Anyway Groome and I are walking to the Step twelve group when we are held up by a newcomer, kicking and screaming she is and I see the perfect opportunity for 'carrying the message' (not the mess). I grab hold of her hand and, looking straight into her eyes, sayz, 'I too is once like you, you need never pick up another drink/drug/whatever . . . there *is* hope!' and off I skip with a glint of fantasticness about me. Dr. Groome puts his hand on my shoulder and sayz, 'Well done.' And the step twelve group is all about people showing off, or, sharing, about carrying the message, not the mess, and going over and over the ground of their own step one so that it could help a newcomer and not because they liked picking at the scab, not because they loved talking about how, they too, were once just a piece of scum, but had been saved by the flowerpot men. And they started to get well into talking about how they saw 'signs' and how their Higher Power, aka God, is talking and working through other people – funny that, I'd have fort He'd come and tell them hisself instead of making it into a treasure hunt of 'signs'! Such a tregateur!

But day 27 arrives. It is here, my dear sistaz.

One more day and I am to be a free . . . whatever, Bill 'N' Bobbite.

Guinea pig.

Then the centre becomes besieged by the Officials. The officials 'we' had voted in, well, not me, but had then proceeded to lie and boss us all around and keep fings going only that is in the interest of their own 'class'. Kunts.

Anyway, I am interviewed, innit.

Asked questions by this Recovery Tsar. Like, 'can you tell us what you were like before you came here?' and I replies, 'Well, I is bad, innit, bad, BUT! Broken, yes, broken, in a million little pieces.'

Aah, the lies.

I want to scream, 'Yeah, I is ANGRY! What's up wiv that? Eh? AND I STILL AM!' but instead I shed a few croc tears and apply to this prompted monologue a liberal sprinkling of Bill 'N' Bob jargon. Like, humility, amends, character defects = defective, etcetera, etcetera, etcetera.

The next morning Fleur comes in with what is to be me last brekkie. No porridge. No muesli. Just a piece of dry toast and a cuppa tea. There is something very different about Fleur this morn. Her hands are still shaking – but not as much. Her shoulders aren't so hunched over either.

'What's up Fleur?' I asks.

'Ooh well, I don't know, I've realised something very important,' she sayz, being careful how much she sayz, 'but, after eight years, I've realised that recovery needn't be worn like a straight jacket, but may suit some worn as a loose overcoat.'

Aaah, aint that nice, a nice 'fitting' analogy. It is obvious she's made the decision to take her new life back *sans* the 'He' God.

The Recovery Tsar makes a big show of signing me, the state's first Bill 'N' Bob guinea pig, out into the 'real' world. I am stood standing in the foyer – one small bag of belongings. Dr. Groome and Mr. Apple are here, looking on with pride at their little meal ticket to greater vanity and ambition. Dr. Groome passes a console towards me and sayz, 'Sign here please Alex, ooh, by the way, it's your birthday today, eighteen, eh?!' he sayz.

My heart sinks.

'My birthday?' asks I.

'Yes. Well, there we are, all signed now, free to go and be good, and remember, tune in to the Recovery Channel – make a date – every night at eight.'

And so I am pushed out of the building with a swipe-card for the bus.

'My birthday?' I asks myself.

I didn't know. I've never celebrated it.

Eighteen? I feels I is much, much older, like, at least nearly thirty or summat.

But eighteen? It feels like the cruelest joke of all – to be told you're just a teenager when you felt like you'd lived the life of an old drudge. Oh well, I sayz to meself, brushing it away, *veni vidi vici*. I'd go check out old Gutshot Rebos – the irony of it, eh? I even fancy taking out my repressed energies and anger on one of those meatheads. Then I'll be off 'home' to Moss-Side, to get my mechanics and balletics out for a good airing. And my darling *La Perla*, white, for my newfound innocence.

'One wheatgrass, straight up,' sez I to the strange girl now serving behind the counter.

'One wheatgrass?' she giggle wiggles.

FOR. FUCKZ. SAKE! Thinks I.

'Yes. One. Wheat.Grass.' sayz I.

'It's so . . . yesterday, it's pomegranate with wheatgerm now,' sayz she.

That's when my face came on all the walls – there I am, 'sharing' oh so humbly with the Recovery Tsar. There is also a voiceover man, saying how this government, that wants so desperately to be given 'another chance', would invest in giving others 'another chance' and thus save society from chavvie types and 'clean up' Moss-Side and make it into a law abiding place. Which really meanz: 'We'll shut 'em up and get 'em to conform like little flocks of lambs . . . so Blytons can show-off without being harassed and feared up.' I then speed down Oxford

Road, towards the old Duchess of New York on McColl where only mumsy wumsy would be.

And indeed she is.

Sat sitting there.

As usual.

Fag in one hand.

Drink in the other.

Gloria and co. are also here, surrounding her on this, what must surely be a difficult day for a woman whose bitch of a daughter, whose eighteenth anniversary of the day of her birth, has today been released, a million years earlier than she had ever thought would be possible.

'Drinkey then, mumsy wumsy,' sayz I.

Her face begins to give way.

Hee hee haw haw. I feel more than a tad weird. I looks over at the bar. Behind is Mid.

'Alex.'

'Mid!'

'Look, yeah . . .' she begins, but her face is no longer the clear healthy it once was. I see opened pores, a spidery scrawl of emerging red thread veins. She's been at the mother's ruin already. And she has a big bump in her belly.

'So. You're to be one of the muvvaz?'

'That's right, things'll be different then, they will.'

'Yeah. Course they will, Mid, course they will.' A slice of silence. The punchline of a dirty joke comes from the muvvaz in the corner and a unison of cackles from that kenspeckle.

'Where's the Drip?' I asks.

'Who? Oh! 'im? He left ages ago,' Mid sayz and picks up a tea-towel to wipe a few ashtrays.

'So, the news sayz that they changed yer, did they?' Gloria pipes up. I turn around.

'FUCK OFF!' sayz I.

Enuff said.

I leave them to it in the old Duchess of New York, armed only with the keys to 'home' – and I don't mind sayin, that, as I come to terms with having to once again living in Moss-Side with old alchie mumsy and the prospect only of workin' in a data input factory my heart sinks in a way that it never ever has before. Sadness knocks on the door. I answer it. It waves. I wave back.

I have to turn it all back into art, I sphinx.

I trudge my formerly light feet past the old Madchester bodyshop – old Moss-Siders are still huddled up against the old gates. Mount Etna is suddenly warming me up. I deliberately walk into a tall figure that passes me; itching for a fight.

A He.

Kunt.

'Ooh, I'm sorry,' sayz he.

I turn round. I know that voice. It is the Drip from the Duchess of New York. It *is* the Drip from the Duchess. He looks . . . different. Solid. ***Select.***

He smiles at me. Not a cheesy grin, but a smile. Of knowing.

I smiles back, without even trying, or meaning to. It's just there. Yare.

'Hey! How are you? How did they treat you?' he asks.

'What the fuck would you care?' sayz I, suddenly shrugging off the smile, but still yare!

'Well. Actually. I did. I used to ask your mum about you, but she never seemed to know anything, so I stopped asking, and then, well, I qualified and was able to leave that old dump, but your old friend, Mid, she took my job, suits her as well,' he sayz. I am in no mood now to talk about Mid, though I do wonder who has really got the worse end of the stick. No doubt I'll see how she progresses with her bambino. Someone'll have to keep a guiding light alive for her, no?

'Qualified as what?'

'Doctor, did you not know? I was at med school for half a lifetime, why else d'ya think I worked in there and took all that crap?'

'Crapola,' I sayz.

'Right. Crapola it is. Was.'

'What's your real name?' I ask.

'Ben,' sez he.

'Ben? Oh!' sayz I. I look down at my shoes. I can feel Etna having moved up from my solar plexus and is now invading my face.

'So, you're out. I saw how the government were exploiting the whole thing and that,' he sayz, digging his hands further into his deep pockets. 'I hope you didn't let them change you too much,' he sayz. I smile again. Unwittingly.

My heart lifts.

D'ya get me?

GLOSSARY

Abalieno –are *(L)* To stay out all night
Abnormis *(L)* Irregular, unconventional
Aboleo *(L)* To destroy/do away with
Aby *(L)* Atone; make amends
animadvertistine, ubicumque stes, fumum recta in faciem ferri *(L)* Ever noticed how wherever you stand, the smoke goes right into your face?
Aegrotat Sick note
Amphigory Nonsense verse – designed to sound/look good but, upon closer study, has no meaning
Alabandical Stupefied from drink; barbarous
Antipelargy Love and care of children for their parents
Aquabib Water-drinker
Auturgy Self-action

Bajulate To bear a heavy burden

Barathrum An abyss; an insatiable person

Blytons Middling/meddling classes

Boustrophedon Writing left to right, then right to left.

Cancrizans To move backwards

Cave ab homine unius libre *(L)* Beware of anyone who has just one book

Cead mile failte A hundred thousand welcomes

Conradh na Gaeilge Organization devoted to the preservation and promotion of the Irish language and culture

Coram *(L)* In the presence of

Delenda Things to be deleted/destroyed (pl.) delere = to delete

Enchiridion Book carried in hand for reference

Episemon Badge

Famulus Servant

Farrago Confused mass of people

Feile Festival

Galimatias Nonsense

Gombeen Moneylender or trader who exploits the disadvantaged through unfair practices

Gregatim *(L)* In flocks

Growlery Retreat for times of ill-humour

Gurrier Juvenile delinquent

Guttatim *(L)* Drop by drop

Haecceity Hereness and nowness – aspect of existence on which individuality depends

Imbroglio Confusing/disturbing situation

Incunabulum An early printed book

Jeremiad Prolonged lamentation/complaint

Kenspeckle Easily distinguishable Alone

Lucubration Study lasting late into the night

Mascaron Grotesque face on door-knocker

Miasma Foul vapours from rotting matter

Mumpsimus View stubbornly held even when shown to be wrong

Nepenthe Drink/drug/other, capable of making one forget suffering

Omphaloskepsis Navel-gazing

Panopticon Prison where all inmates can be seen from one point

Peccavi Admission of sin/guilt

Phrontistery Thinking place

Pilgarlick Poor wretch

Punctatim *(L)* Point by point

Rhadamanthine Rigorously just and severe

Seanachai Story-teller

Selcouth Strange, unfamiliar, marvellous

Shebeen Illegal drinking den, from the Irish sibin.

Singillatim *(L)* Singly

Sisyphean Laborious, endless and futile

Solus *(L)* Solitary Alone

Tantivy At full gallop

Tintinnabulate To ring / tinkle

Tregateur Trickster / deceiver

Ubique *(L)* Everywhere

Ultracrepidate To criticize beyond sphere of one's knowledge

Variorum *(L)* Including notes of earlier scholars or editors

Veni Vidi Vici *(L)* I came, I saw, I conquered

Vilipend To despise

Widdershins In contrary direction

Yare Prompt/nimble/prepared

Zeteticism Withholding belief until evidence - opposite of cynicism